Dialogue w
the long-aw:
Darcy's Story ~~by Janet Aylmer~~

"Pride and Prejudice" from
the hero's point of view.

More than 150,000 copies sold.

Dialogue with Darcy is an interesting and
entertaining book about the first period of
the marriage between Darcy and Elizabeth,
and his continuing progress
towards improved self knowledge
and lasting happiness.

Darcy has always prided himself
on his ability to advise his friends
and family on their relationships
and decisions in life,
preferring his personal judgement
in such matters to their own wishes.

His recent marriage to Elizabeth Bennet
has not altered his confidence about
his own superior competence
in such matters.

It takes Darcy some time to discover that
his dear wife has at least
as sound an ability to judge
situations and human frailties as he does,
and to understand that
her solutions can often be
much more successful than his own.

Janet Aylmer is an English author who
enjoys reading historical romances
set in the early 1800s.

Her favourite writer is Georgette Heyer,
whose stories feature the trials and
tribulations of a lively heroine
and a handsome hero
living in the turbulent times when
Jane Austen was writing
her famous novels

Books by Janet Aylmer

Darcy's Story (UK 1996, HarperCollins USA
2006)

The new Illustrated Darcy's Story (1999)

**Walking with Jane Austen through Bath to
Widcombe & Lyncombe** (2003)

Julia & the Master of Morancourt

(HarperCollins USA 2009)

Sophie's Salvation (2015)

Dialogue with Darcy (2015)

From the author of **Darcy's Story**
(more than 150,000 copies sold)

A Sequel

Dialogue with Darcy

by

Janet Aylmer

ISBN 978-0-9528210-4-5

Published by Copperfield Books, Tunbridge Wells

Printed and bound by CPI Group (UK) Ltd,
Croydon, CR0 4YY

This book is for the very many people

who enjoyed reading Darcy's Story

and for Ali and Joel

CHAPTER ONE

Sitting at his desk in the library, Darcy looked out of the window. However, his eyes did not really see the familiar view over the lake at Pemberley. Instead, in the forefront of his mind was the soft touch of Elizabeth's fingers on his when he had left her at the door to the terrace only a few minutes ago, and his memory of that secret smile that she kept only for him.

On the other side of the library, Colonel Fitzwilliam was standing with a book in his hand, looking rather less calm than usual. He might be a guest in his cousin's house, but that did not mean that he had to agree with everything that Darcy said.

His host had always prided himself on his ability to advise his friends and family about their lives. That he was not inclined to take any notice of what they might suggest was not something to which Darcy ever gave much attention.

"After all, Fitzwilliam, we have already agreed that it is essential for you to marry well, for your future financial security. So what is the problem? I cannot see any difficulty."

His cousin sighed. Why was it that Darcy suddenly became deaf to any rational discussion if one held an opposite view to his own? He had hoped that his cousin's happy alliance with Elizabeth would mean an improved understanding on Darcy's part about personal matters. Marriage, after all, was one of the most important steps in life that anyone had to take, and his own lack of a settled income made it

1

particularly necessary that the decision should be given great care.

The irritation that Darcy felt about his cousin's attitude was tempered by his pleasure in seeing his new wife Elizabeth sitting outside in the sunshine, reading one of the books that she had brought with her from her father's library. It did not seem so long ago that he had feared he might never be able to persuade her to marry him. But now their settled future lay ahead, the very real prospect of a family of his own, and the support of the person that he loved most in all the world.

However, a slight movement by his cousin reminded him of his duty. He had not hesitated to speak to Colonel Fitzwilliam about his future marriage plans. After all, the colonel was a close relative and was now nearly thirty years of age. As the younger son of an earl, he might not have significant financial prospects, but he was very well connected socially, quite apart from being Darcy's own first cousin. In addition, he was tall, had a distinguished appearance and a very pleasant personal manner.

"Surely you really must agree that my suggestion is the best solution for both of you." Darcy had been very irritated that the colonel had not shared his initial enthusiasm for the idea.

Colonel Fitzwilliam took a deep breath, and repeated what he had said to Darcy several times before.

"Of course, she is a most delightful young woman and, as you have reminded me, we have known each other for a long time, indeed ever since she was born. But why should Georgiana see me as a potential partner in life? She has a handsome dowry, as you have so often told me, and that would attract many men with a more substantial income and at least as elevated a social situation as myself, and who could offer her much more comfortable circumstances."

Dialogue with Darcy

"That may be so, Fitzwilliam, but she has shown very little interest to date in any of the young men to whom she has been introduced, despite the best efforts of myself, and more recently my dear wife. If Elizabeth cannot persuade Georgiana that any of them are worthy of her consideration, then has it occurred to you that she might be harbouring a secret passion for someone else, for you?"

Colonel Fitzwilliam looked at him with a weary expression. There were times when Darcy behaved in a very similar way to their aunt Lady Catherine de Bourgh, who could be so high-handed as to alienate not only her acquaintances, but also her immediate family. Yet Darcy was even less inclined than most people to do what others suggested to him.

"As far as I can tell, Georgiana is not harbouring what you call a secret passion for anyone, and certainly not for me. For heaven's sake, Darcy, where is the urgency for you to have to find her a partner in life?"

The colonel walked over to look out of the window at the view outside. On the sunny terrace, Elizabeth was now getting up to join her sister-in-law standing by the lake, and soon they were busy in animated conversation. He was sure that Elizabeth would have rather different views about her husband's suggestion, and perhaps it was time for him to take her aside and discuss the matter in private.

"Would you like me to have a word with my sister on your behalf?" said Darcy.

"No, I would not," his cousin hastily replied, "that would be premature, to say the least. In any case, I have no need of you to make my addresses for me, and I wish to consider the subject much more carefully before I do anything."

Darcy sighed, and picked up his pen to continue the letter that he had been writing, and Colonel Fitzwilliam turned on his heel, and left.

Dialogue with Darcy

Later that afternoon, he found Elizabeth in her sitting room on the first floor, and decided to broach the matter without any further delay. He explained what Darcy had said, and what his own reservations were.

Elizabeth motioned for the colonel to sit down in the chair opposite her.

"I do wish that my dear Mr. Darcy would allow other people to make their own decisions, and not forget that sometimes they might do better to follow their personal preferences. Georgiana is perfectly capable of making up her own mind about who she wants to marry, and there is absolutely no hurry, for she has only just reached eighteen years of age. It would be most unfortunate if my dear husband were to blunder about, upsetting everyone, just because he thinks that two of his relatives marrying each other would be an ideal and tidy solution to what only he perceives as urgent problems."

The colonel smiled. If Elizabeth was less enamoured of the idea than Darcy, then there was hope for a more satisfactory outcome. His cousin had been transformed in so many ways by his marriage a few months ago, and was altogether a much more relaxed and contented man than he had ever been previously. Colonel Fitzwilliam knew that Elizabeth was very fond of her new sister-in-law, and was very unlikely to want to do anything that would make her unhappy.

"Do you think that you can persuade Darcy to direct his attention to some other, more pressing, concerns – something on the Pemberley estates, for instance?"

She smiled again. "I will try, and shall do so, as long as you assure me that there is no likelihood of your changing your mind about Georgiana?"

"I will not be doing that. As I have no sisters of my own, I have always valued Georgiana as very close to being my sister by birth, but not as a potential wife!"

Elizabeth decided to change the subject and follow his suggestion.

"Perhaps what we all really need is something to divert our attention. Why don't we all make an expedition tomorrow to Buxton? I hear that there is to be a demonstration there of a new high pressure steam engine. That is just the kind of thing that will divert my dear Darcy and give him something else to think about. Are you willing to accompany us, Fitzwilliam? I am sure that Georgiana would welcome an outing."

Gratefully, he agreed to the suggestion and, as Elizabeth had anticipated, her husband and sister-in-law were happy to complete the party.

The family's carriage was well sprung, and so they had a comfortable drive to the handsome stone built town built on the slopes of the valley of the River Wye. Georgiana joined happily in the family's conversation during the journey, but showed no inclination that Elizabeth could discern to single out Colonel Fitzwilliam for special attention. As for any secret passion by Georgiana for Fitzwilliam as Darcy had suggested to his wife when they retired to bed the night before, Elizabeth thought that was totally unlikely.

The demonstration was to be in the park at Buxton and, by the time their carriage came to a halt, quite a crowd of people had assembled, waiting to see the new innovation. The inventor and his engineer were busy making their final preparations, and various citizens from the town had already taken their places around the high pressure machine.

Darcy and Colonel Fitzwilliam went forward to look more closely at the front of the steam engine, where a large cylindrical barrel was being filled with more water. Elizabeth and Georgiana stayed where they were, on a grassy slope overlooking the scene where they had a good view of the proceedings.

Elizabeth was rather taken aback when Georgiana suddenly addressed her in an uncharacteristically blunt manner.

"Elizabeth, has my brother said anything to you about our dear cousin Fitzwilliam? I suspect that he has some stupid scheme to create an alliance between us. I had hoped that his marriage to you would have persuaded him to mind his own business and stop trying to organise my life!"

A delightful smile overtook Elizabeth's face in the way that had so originally enchanted Mr. Darcy. Her eyes sparkled as she replied to the enquiry.

"You are, as ever, perfectly correct about your brother. Yes, for some reason best known to my dear husband, he has indeed decided that an alliance between you would be a splendid idea. Do not doubt, Georgiana, that I am of the opinion that both you and Colonel Fitzwilliam will find married happiness elsewhere with someone quite different, and unconnected with our family."

Georgiana relaxed, and squeezed Elizabeth's hand in gratitude. However much she loved her brother, to have an ally so close in the family was such a relief, and made her life considerably easier.

"Perhaps we could persuade Darcy to invest in the steam engine, and some other modern innovations. I often think that, with the help of his factor, his estates run so smoothly that he needs some new distraction to keep him busy."

"Do you mind my asking, Georgiana, whether you have ever found yourself with a preference for any of the young men whom you have met?"

Georgiana blushed slightly, and turned her head away for a moment before replying.

"There was recently someone, the younger son of a family that we had known for many years, who did seem more agreeable than others. However, I am very anxious not to disclose this to my brother, for reasons that I do not need to spell out to you. The moment that he has any idea about any prospective suitor, he is sure to rush in and spoil everything for me!"

Elizabeth hesitated to reply to this confidence for a few moments, and eventually said quietly to Georgiana that they must discuss the subject at some other more suitable time, in a more private location.

The sudden escalation of the noise from the steam engine took their attention back to the scene before them, and slowly the engine rumbled into motion, observed closely by the crowd of people standing on the track through the park. Darcy and Fitzwilliam by this time were amongst a group of gentlemen who were walking on the far side of the steam engine as it began to operate, emitting a series of blasts from its chimney as it did so. Eventually the steam ceased to rise from the machine into the sky just below Elizabeth and Georgiana.

When Darcy and Fitzwilliam had rejoined them, Elizabeth enquired what information they had gained about the new invention. Her husband launched into a detailed explanation of the technical arrangements, with Colonel Fitzwilliam intervening from time to time to give added detail.

"That is enough for now," laughed Elizabeth, "for I am sure that I cannot force any more facts into my head. If you are really so interested, why do you not invite the inventor to bring the machine to give us a demonstration at Pemberley?"

Neither she nor Georgiana were surprised when Darcy explained that he had already done so, and that the infernal machine might be brought to the estate before too long for them to examine more closely.

Dialogue with Darcy

On the journey home, the two gentlemen engaged in an animated discussion about the high pressure engine whilst Elizabeth and her sister-in-law talked of more domestic matters. Later that night, when Darcy and Elizabeth had retired to their room, she took the opportunity to bring up the subject of Colonel Fitzwilliam's future.

"Please humour me in this, dear Mr. Darcy. The colonel is a fine young man, and perfectly capable of deciding for himself who he should marry. Georgiana regards him as a brother, not a potential suitor, so please do not cause unnecessary dissension in your - no, our - family by suggesting otherwise."

Darcy was inclined to disagree, but the prospect of arguing with Elizabeth did not appeal. He embraced her and said quietly, "I can think of so many other more delightful occupations for us both this evening than arranging the future happiness of Georgiana and Colonel Fitzwilliam."

Elizabeth was beginning to know Darcy well enough not to be surprised to find that this was only a temporary respite from his desire to arrange his family's affairs. On several occasions during the next few days, her husband raised the subject with her again, but she persisted in her view and persuaded him that he would be better to transfer his time and attention to the imminent arrival of the steam engine.

Georgiana and Colonel Fitzwilliam continued their normal cousinly relationship, and he decided to resist the idea of raising the subject of their future partners with her. He knew Georgiana well enough to know that she was perfectly capable of discussing the matter with him if she desired to do so. He did not have so many relations that he really valued that he was willing to risk upsetting someone whose company he enjoyed in a non-romantic way.

Dialogue with Darcy

Meanwhile, Elizabeth was trying to remember who it might be that Georgiana had in mind when she had referred to a young man who had interested her. The Darcy family had a wide acquaintance within Derbyshire, although in the few months of her marriage so far Elizabeth had only had the opportunity to meet some of them. It did not seem likely, since Georgiana shared her brother's fastidious attitude to people in some respects, that the young man in question would be just anyone, without very special personal qualities.

"Tell me," she said playfully to Georgiana one day, "what are your ideal requirements in a suitor? Would they include character, or ambition, or his physical attributes, or financial circumstances, or his social connections? Which of those are most significant to you, dear sister?"

Georgiana did not hesitate in her reply, smiling as she did so. "All of them, of course, Elizabeth. But, to be more serious, personal character must be the most important, for my dowry indicates that financial circumstances need not be crucial. And I am sure that you would agree that physical attributes can sometimes conceal an inadequate character."

Elizabeth had no difficulty in concur in with that, for she could recall many pleasant young men with a handsome exterior whose personalities left a great deal to be desired. She could remember her mother being unreasonably influenced by tall gentlemen with a reliable income who she herself had found impossibly boring and totally unattractive in their persons.

"I have noticed," said Georgiana shyly, "that sometimes my dear brother is just content to hold your hand when you are together, without saying anything. That is so unlike him that I assume that touching a person you love feels wonderful!"

Elizabeth found herself lost for words. How could you explain to someone who had probably not yet experienced the same emotions that being in love had turned her world upside down, so that nothing mattered for her except being with her dear Darcy, and happily it seemed that he felt exactly the same?

"When you fall in love, dear Georgiana, you will not need an explanation, for you will know exactly why being with the person you care for so much is more important than anything else in the world."

"That sounds so wonderful; I do hope that I am as fortunate as you when the time comes."

The following day, the arrival of the steam engine diverted all other thoughts from their minds. Elizabeth and Georgiana had made arrangements to provide the inventor and his engineer with a light luncheon after their journey and, before the meal, Georgiana fell into conversation with the inventor's assistant. He was a fair-haired young man with a slight Scottish accent, who appeared to be very knowledgeable about the steam engine and had the happy ability to explain how it worked to the ladies in a way that they could easily understand.

"Why is it, Mr. Fraser, that so much water is needed to propel the machine into motion? For that, in turn, must mean that the barrel of the engine has to be very large, and increase the weight of the whole apparatus?"

Darcy, listening to his sister's question, was amazed at her ability to rationalise the requirements that had to be balanced in order for the engine to operate effectively. Colonel Fitzwilliam, standing opposite him, had to exert himself to conceal his amusement. Georgiana meanwhile, oblivious to her brother's expression, continue to enquire of Mr. Fraser other details of the machine, and its intended use.

Elizabeth, entering the room, invited the inventor and his colleague Mr. Brown to join them at luncheon before the full demonstration of what the steam engine could do.

Sitting next to his hostess, Mr. Fraser continued in his detailed explanations. How interesting, she thought, that Georgiana finds all this is so intriguing when there is a limit to what I myself need to know. Colonel Fitzwilliam, on the far side of Mr. Fraser, was of a similar opinion. At the end of the table, Darcy was having an intense conversation with the inventor, and Fitzwilliam soon decided that his cousin was seriously considering making an investment in the machine with a view to its further development for purposes on the Pemberley estate.

When the visitors had gone, Georgiana was in the library with her brother, and found herself in receipt of the conversation that she had been trying so frequently to avoid. At least, she thought, I have had plenty of time to compose my reply.

"Darcy, I am not interested in Colonel Fitzwilliam in the way you like to suggest. He is a charming and well liked cousin as far as I am concerned, a close relative and part of our family, but I do not wish to marry someone who is a friend. I want my future partner in life to really interest me in a personal way, who can bring something new to my life, and create an independent and loving partnership just like that which you and Elizabeth now enjoy. Be honest, you would not have thanked me to try to arrange your own matrimony!"

"But my dear Georgiana ..."

"I am not your dear Georgiana, Darcy! I want, one day, to be someone else's dear Georgiana, someone of my own choice. Please do not upset me any further by raising the subject, which as far as I'm concerned is closed."

On the way out of the library, Georgiana passed Elizabeth entering the room, and her

11

expression left her sister-in-law in no doubt what the discussion had been about.

Before Elizabeth could say anything, Darcy put his head in his hands and then looked up at her.

"Why will she not do as I say?"

"Perhaps, my dear sir, because she has good judgement and is old enough now to know her own mind. Please, my love, do cease to meddle. I do so hate arguments in this house and, be honest, so do you."

He smiled at her ruefully, and then took her hand and held it gently against his cheek in that loving gesture that never failed to make her heart race.

The steam engine had been housed for a few days in a disused stable at the rear of the property. Mr. Brown, who they had discovered was a distant relative of the engineer, now returned alone with some modifications that had been created at the request of Mr. Darcy. They spent several hours in the stables, with the help of one of the grooms, adjusting the performance of the machine until it was running to their satisfaction.

Then the rest of the family was called to observe the steam machine being fired up in the yard.

"I must admit that the engine can be remarkably noisy," said Elizabeth, "when it is placed on a hard surface. But maybe that is partly because it is echoing the noise against the stone walls on each side. I do wonder whether it is likely to frighten the horses or the cattle on the estate if it is to be used anywhere near them."

"That is true, my dear, but it will not normally be employed in that location or so close to the house."

The inventor explained, with the help of Mr. Darcy, that his host's intention was that the machine could assist in pumping water from the river and the lake for the animals, and in driving other machinery to sharpen tools and farming implements used on the Pemberley estate.

Elizabeth noticed that Georgiana was taking less interest in the activities today than when Mr. Fraser had been present on the previous occasion. She enquired of the inventor where his colleague was, and was told that he was busy elsewhere, assisting another landowner who had purchased a machine in adapting it for his particular purposes.

When she had the opportunity, Elizabeth asked Mr. Brown how he and Mr. Fraser had originally become interested in matters mechanical, and the development of the steam engine. Mr. Brown explained that Mr. Fraser was the younger son of a well-connected Scottish family. After completing his education at St Andrews' University, he had gone against the wishes of his family in pursuing his particular interest in the use of steam in manufacture and for other purposes. When Mr. Brown had constructed his first steam engine, Mr. Fraser had moved from Scotland to live in Manchester, so that he could take a more active part in the development of the machine.

"That is all very interesting, my dear, but I really think that such subjects are not really appropriate for a lady's ears."

Colonel Fitzwilliam, standing nearby, could see Elizabeth's expression and waited for the explosion to come at her husband's remark. But she, returning his look, controlled her irritation and replied sweetly that what was suitable would rather depend on which lady he might be talking about.

"Perhaps you could explain to me, dear sir," said Colonel Fitzwilliam, "whether you think it likely that many people may be interested in purchasing this engine. I can understand its application for what Darcy wants to achieve, but I believe that there are machines being developed elsewhere in the country that might compete with this one."

The inventor agreed with his remark, and said that it was necessary to constantly adapt the steam engine to stay ahead of innovations elsewhere. After a few more alterations, Darcy and Mr. Brown both pronounced themselves satisfied with its performance, and the inventor said his farewells.

After this unusual diversion, life at Pemberley resumed its normal pattern, with visits to friends in the locality, and expeditions to Lambton, the local small town, for Elizabeth and Georgiana to make some personal purchases.

"It is so enjoyable for me to have your company, Elizabeth. I became so tired of having no one with whom to share my interests, and there were often very few young ladies of my own age in this part of Derbyshire, since they might be in London or away at school, as I had been for a time. I know that you have four sisters, so I assume that you never had the same problem."

"Well, perhaps, but only Jane and I are really of a like mind. Mary, Kitty and Lydia have always had very different interests. Darcy always likes to be right, as you know, and in one respect he was correct - in hoping that you and I should become close friends."

Georgiana laughed and agreed.

"But if you are suggesting, dear sister, that he is more interested in that than having your constant company, I do not believe you. You cannot know, of course, how solitary a person he used to be before he met you. I often used to worry about my brother because he seemed to be so lonely. The transformation gives me pleasure every day that I see you together with him!"

These heartfelt remarks quite removed Elizabeth's ability to make a coherent reply in words, so instead she gave her sister-in-law a loving embrace which she hoped expressed her feelings.

Meanwhile, Darcy and his cousin Fitzwilliam kept well occupied on the estate, and went out regularly to shoot the birds on the grouse moor. That was not an occupation of which either Elizabeth or Georgiana really approved, but it was best not to make their views too obvious, since shooting was such a common pastime for the young men in wellborn families. At least they could produce some birds for the pot, to supplement the other foods produced on the estate or purchased in Lambton, the nearby town, or in Buxton or Manchester.

Subsequently, Darcy only mentioned the subject of marriage once more to his cousin, and with no more success than before, for Fitzwilliam was adamant in his opinions.

"I am sorry, Darcy, but I do not wish to raise the subject with Georgiana at all. We are good friends, but no more than that. One day I will meet someone and fall impossibly in love. You can only hope that it is with someone who is an heiress, or is willing to live with me in genteel poverty!"

Darcy did not really approve of this unseemly levity on such an important subject, but had the justice to admit that he had brought it upon himself.

"Very well, dear cousin. I shall say no more about it, at least for now."

Then, seeing Fitzwilliam's very resolute expression, he said, "No, I mean until you raise the matter yourself with me, and not otherwise."

When Colonel Fitzwilliam discussed this conversation with Elizabeth later in the week, she observed that this last sentence was, for Darcy, a really major concession, and indicated some progress in his education about what should and should not concern him.

Then his hostess, anxious to change the subject, held up the letter in her hand and said, "I have something here that will give Mr. Darcy plenty to think about. My mother is proposing that she should pay us a visit sometime in the next few weeks. This is not an idea that either Darcy or I would welcome, but I fear that it cannot be postponed very much longer. My Papa was here only a month ago, and in any case is unlikely to accompany her. He will always be a welcome guest, but a visit from my other dear parent is most unlikely to be as restful."

"Perhaps it would be just as well to get it over with? Sometimes the anticipation is worse than the event?"

"You may be right. The visit will probably go much better if I can find something to keep my mother well entertained whilst she is here, so that she does not busy herself trying to alter our domestic arrangements or take over our social life. Do you have any suggestions as to what I might propose to keep my dear Mama fully occupied for a few days? She is always more pleasant company when she has plenty to do."

"Yes, indeed that may be true, and perhaps not only for Mrs. Bennet. Surely there are many families in the village that would be grateful for her attention? I know you attend to such matters yourself, but surely there could be no unfortunate consequences if she were to assist you for a short time? Does she take any interest in the cultivation of village plots for vegetables? I can recall that my mother the Countess, when she was younger, encouraged the family's tenants to grow as much of their own food as they could, so that they did not have to go to the market to make expensive purchases from others."

Elizabeth agreed that this might indeed be a good plan, and likely to occupy her mother for some time.

When his wife brought the contents of Mrs. Bennet's letter to his attention, Mr. Darcy's reaction was as she had expected – a mixture of rather formal politeness and a lack of enthusiasm. However, he agreed with Elizabeth that the visit could not really be postponed any longer. Provided that a fixed duration was specified in her reply, he was willing to endure what was likely to be a less than enjoyable few days.

"I have only met your Mama once, I think", said Georgiana later in the day, "at your wedding, so I shall be pleased to have a further opportunity to make her acquaintance. I'm sure", she said carefully, "that she is more agreeable than my brother would wish to admit."

Elizabeth agreed with her that this must be so, and together they both began to devise a programme of excursions to keep Mrs. Bennet busy during her forthcoming visit. There were a few, just a few, friends and acquaintances, Elizabeth thought who could be invited to meet her mother without reporting all her foibles to all the gentry in the county. Equally, there were some individuals who should on no account be introduced to Mrs. Bennet during her stay.

Colonel Fitzwilliam, on hearing of the impending arrival of the lady, decided to make his excuses and travel south to visit his brother, the Earl, for a week or two. It was clear that Mr. Darcy would have liked to do the same. He looked for any sign that Georgiana would miss the company of their cousin, but even he could not discern any regret in her conduct or conversation which would support that view.

Dialogue with Darcy

CHAPTER TWO

Because of the early death of his mother, and his father's rather reserved personality, Darcy had had no experience for many years of feeling cared for by another person. He continued to enjoy a happy relationship with his younger sister Georgiana, but that had always been in the context of the ten year gap between them in age, and their differing interests.

So it had come as a delightful surprise to him to experience the pleasure of his marriage with his new wife Elizabeth. Her lively manner and expressive way of speaking were not unexpected following on their early acquaintance, but her interest in his ideas and plans, and learning more about his various pursuits, were very gratifying.

She was affectionate towards him in so many small ways, so that few hours passed in the day without a smile or some other token of her affection, showing him that he was the centre of her world.

"Do you mind," she once asked him shyly, "if I touch your hand, just now and then? That makes me feel much closer to you."

Darcy did not answer her, but instead took her hand and held it close to his cheek before kissing her palm, and the tips of each of her fingers. Elizabeth blushed before reciprocating his gesture.

"I must admit that one of the reasons why I'm not looking forward to the visit from Mrs Bennet is that we shall lose most of our personal privacy whilst she is here at Pemberley."

19

"Yes, I feel the same, but I do try to remember that she is my mother, and I owe her a great deal, and that she always believes that she is acting in the best interests of myself and all her children."

Darcy thought to himself, not for the first time, that Mrs Bennet's persistence was a characteristic that her daughter had inherited. But Elizabeth's considerable intellectual capacity clearly came from her father's side of the family, as well as her very lively sense of humour, for which he was usually very grateful.

"Would I be right in saying that your mother rarely enjoys a joke, especially against herself?"

Elizabeth grimaced, and acknowledged that he was quite correct.

"I hope that you will tell me at any time during her stay if there are any particular problems for you, my dearest. I promise that I shall do my best not to allow myself to be provoked whilst Mrs Bennet is here, for after all we shall have the opportunity ourselves for private moments in our bedchamber every evening after she has retired to bed."

His wife smiled shyly at him, and agreed, and resolved to control her own temper, for she was well aware that her own patience might be sorely tried during her mother's forthcoming visit.

It had been agreed that Mr Darcy would go in the carriage to Derby on the following day to meet the stagecoach from the South, and bring his mother-in-law on the last stage of her journey to Pemberley.

After her prompt arrival, Mrs. Bennet scarcely allowed any time to elapse after supervising the unpacking of her trunks in the bedchamber before she insisted in being shown the main reception rooms. Her mother's initial reactions to the glories of Pemberley were as effusive as her daughter Elizabeth had anticipated. Every detail of the furnishings, the magnificent drapes at the windows, and the ornamentation of the ceilings in the mansion were remarked on favourably.

Elizabeth had made sure that Mr. Darcy was not present for more than part of the time during this process of inspection, and when he was most likely to be able to maintain an admirable level of composure. Only when they were alone in their bed chamber at night did he allow himself any comments.

"I had forgotten, my dear, how your Mama needs to endorse every aspect of life in someone else's home and pronounce it to her satisfaction. I am waiting with bated breath for her to suggest some necessary improvements, perhaps to my library, or to the ballroom?"

"That can only be a matter of time, sir, but pray do not allow my mother's preferences to affect your own judgement!"

Had not the saucy expression on his wife's face reminded him of particular occasions during their courtship, Darcy might have been offended, but instead he took it as an opportunity to remind her of her filial duty to take Mrs. Bennet's comments seriously.

"But I am, my dear Mr. Darcy, I am. And I know how much in need you are of advice on how to decorate and furnish the house where you and your family have lived for so many years!"

When Elizabeth took her mother to see the portrait gallery on the first floor, Mrs. Bennet was mightily impressed by the rows of oil paintings of previous generations of the family that dated back more than two hundred and fifty years, to the reign of the Tudor monarch Queen Elizabeth. When she reached the picture of Mr. Darcy's father, she stopped and remarked on the similarities in their facial expressions. However, she could not discern any likeness in another portrait between Darcy's late mother and her sister, Lady Catherine de Bourgh.

"She has a much more pleasant expression than that lady could ever achieve, Lizzy, I'm sure."

"My husband tells me," Elizabeth replied, "that they were very different in character. His aunt is the eldest in the family, followed by her brother the Earl of __, with Darcy's mother being very much younger."

Mrs. Bennet moved on to a portrait of her son in law, which she was told had been painted some five years earlier.

"I would not say that the picture favours him, my dear! That very severe expression does him little credit, or perhaps the artist did not create an accurate likeness? Is Mr. Darcy planning for a portrait to be painted of you, Lizzy?"

"We have discussed the subject once or twice, Mama. I would prefer an artist to create a picture of both of us, as was done for the oil painting of Darcy's grandfather and his wife that you saw earlier."

This answer seemed to satisfy her mother's curiosity and, after commending the quality of a delightful watercolour of a younger Miss Georgiana Darcy at the end of the gallery, they moved on to view other parts of the house.

It had been agreed that Mrs. Bennet could only be spared by Mr. Bennet from her home in Hertfordshire for a few days, and it took fully two of those for her to inspect all the glories of the house at Pemberley. An expedition to Lambton, the small local town, occupied another few hours and, when the weather improved, Elizabeth took her Mama on a drive around the extensive grounds of the estate to see views of the hills in the area known as The Peak.

"What a delightful county this is, Lizzy! I am so sad that I have never previously had the opportunity to visit Derbyshire."

The next day, what initially had seemed to be another quite simple idea by Elizabeth to give her mother something to occupy her almost escalated into a major expedition.

She had arranged for her dear Mama to be accompanied to the estate cottages on the Lambton Road by the under gardener who was in charge of the kitchen garden at Pemberley. Followed by one of the garden boys with a well laden wheelbarrow, Mrs. Bennet made her way up the path leading to one of the properties, where the under gardener had already knocked on the door.

A rather flustered elderly woman opened the door so promptly that she had clearly been forewarned about the unusual visitor. She did not admit Mrs. Bennet to the cottage, perhaps embarrassed by its simple furnishings. Instead, she came outside and invited her guest to go round the back of the property, where an overgrown vegetable plot could be found.

It was some two hours later that Elizabeth took the short journey in one of the carriages and arrived at the cottage to see what progress was being made. Getting no answer when she knocked on the front door, she walked round the end of the property to find a rather chaotic scene. It was immediately clear that her Mama had not confined herself to supervising the introduction of plants that had been carried in the wheelbarrow from the Pemberley kitchen garden onto the limited area of ground required for that particular purpose.

Instead, the whole plot had been dug over, albeit in a rather hasty fashion, and the under gardener was leaning wearily on his spade surveying his handiwork, and supervising the garden boy, who was completing the task of putting in the last few vegetable plants.

The cottage's elderly tenant was standing at the further end of the plot, looking bemused, and with an untidy pile of weeds and old vegetable plants just behind her. Whatever she had expected to happen had clearly been exceeded by the visitors.

"Are you making good progress, Mama?" asked Elizabeth cautiously, and trying to hide her amusement.

"Of course, my dear," said her mother decisively. "I regret to say that there was some initial resistance from this persons to my proposal that we dig over the entire plot," pointing at the unfortunate resident of the property, "but I explained to her that all the plants that we had brought with us would do much better if the bed was dug over completely before the new ones were put into the soil."

From the under gardener's expression, Elizabeth suspected that the story was rather more complicated than that, but this did not seem the right moment to make further enquiries. So she contented herself with explaining that she had bought one of the family's carriages with her, so that her Mama did not need to fatigue herself any further by making the return journey on foot. Elizabeth took pity on the under gardener by proposing that he also accompany them in the carriage, despite his protestations that his boots were very muddy, since that problem could be overcome by handing them to the garden boy to bring back in a wheelbarrow at a leisurely pace.

When they had all returned to the mansion at Pemberley, and Mrs. Bennet had been persuaded to rest in her room until it was time for dinner, Elizabeth sought out Darcy to give him an account of the expedition.

"So my unfortunate tenant had very little say in the matter, my dearest, from what you have just told me. Is it likely that those plants will in fact be looked after until maturity, or will the vegetable plot now revert to its previous un-cared for condition? The woman is a widow getting on in years, I understand, and not in the best of health."

Dialogue with Darcy

Elizabeth smiled and replied, "I rather doubt if any of that matters very much, since my mother will have returned home to Longbourn several months before we know the answer to those questions. In the meantime, my idea has served its purpose, or at least I hope so."

In the ensuing days, Mrs. Bennet had to be dissuaded from inflicting the same treatment on the residents in all the other cottages. However, Elizabeth was able to find two who were willing to accept some contributions to their vegetable plots, and this time she persuaded her mother to confine her supervision to inspecting the final results that the under gardener had achieved.

However, it was on one of those occasions that Mrs. Bennet was able to be of real use – something that was always close to her heart. The woman occupying the last cottage had several small children, one of whom was clearly not in good health. She was reluctant to bring the small girl outside into the light, but Mrs. Bennet insisted. After a short examination of the rash covering the child's face and arms, she pronounced her opinion that it might well be measles or scarlet fever, and that the doctor should be called straight away.

"I can't afford to pay for a doctor to visit, ma'am," said the mother wearily.

"Nonsense," said Mrs. Bennet, "I or if necessary Mr. Darcy will pay for that," and she sent the under gardener back to Pemberley immediately to ask for help to be summoned.

By the time that Elizabeth and Mr. Darcy heard about the emergency, the doctor had been brought across from Lambton to examine the child, and had agreed that Mrs. Bennet's diagnosis of measles was correct. He prescribed some appropriate medicine, and promised to return in a few days to monitor progress.

Mrs. Bennet was unexpectedly deferential when she discussed the subject with her new son-in-law.

Dialogue with Darcy

"I do hope, Mr. Darcy, that you did not mind my intervening in the matter, but I have been told that it is essential not to delay with that kind of sickness. I'm quite willing to pay the visit from the doctor if you would like me to do so."

For once, Darcy regarded Mrs. Bennet with a benevolent expression and, whilst thanking her for her kind suggestion, said that he would be very happy to bear the cost of the visit, and any subsequent ones that might be required to bring the child back to health.

If Elizabeth had hoped that this pleasant conversation meant that the remaining days of the visit would pass without incident, unhappily she was to be disappointed. She had realised from the day of her mother's arrival that Georgiana's normally sunny disposition was being sorely tested by the comments being made by the visitor about the need to consider her marriage prospects without delay.

"I am so sorry to have to complain to you, dear Elizabeth, but I really do not think that it is seemly for Mrs. Bennet to make remarks like that. That subject has absolutely nothing to do with her, and I should be most grateful if you could persuade her to concentrate on some other topic of conversation when we are in the same room."

Elizabeth could not agree more, and took her Mama aside to explain exactly that.

The effort of maintaining her veneer of polite interest in Pemberley and its occupants was beginning to be too much for Mrs. Bennet, and she rounded angrily on her second daughter.

"I suppose that you are suggesting that my opinion is not good enough for Miss Georgiana Darcy and her grand surroundings! If she were my daughter, Lizzy, I would not allow her to be languishing here, buried in the country and far away from all the eligible young men in town! If she is not very careful, she will be left on the shelf and become an old maid like that ugly daughter of Lady Catherine de Bourgh!"

"Really, Mama, there can be no comparison between dear Georgiana and the daughter of Lady Catherine. That is like suggesting that chalk and cheese are the same! There is no need to concern yourself about Georgiana's marriage prospects when she is still so young."

"Young! Why she is nearly two years older than my dear Lydia when she was married to Mr. Wickham last year! What are you thinking of?"

Anxious not to prolong this discussion, her daughter suggested that Mrs. Bennet accompany her to Elizabeth's dressing room, to inspect two of the new gowns that had recently been made for her by one of the best dressmakers in Manchester.

After admiring the quality and style of the pale pink silk dress with lace trimmings, Mrs. Bennet asked how far it was to travel to that town.

After Elizabeth had explained that it was a journey of about forty miles, her mother replied forcefully, "Such a distance, my dear Lizzy? Could you not find a dressmaker of quality closer to Pemberley?"

One of those secret smiles that Darcy liked so much passed quickly across Elizabeth's face as she replied, "There was no need for that, Mama. Georgiana has used Madame Veronique for some years to make many of her dresses, and she will travel here to Pemberley to take our order if we need more than one gown to be made at one time."

This statement mightily impressed Mrs. Bennet, although she decided not to admit the fact, but stored up the remark to repeat it to Lady Lucas in Meryton immediately on her return to Hertfordshire.

"So what else did you order from Madame Veronique on that occasion, my dear Lizzy?"

Dialogue with Darcy

"I chose this evening gown, in apricot figured silk with a train, ready to wear at one of the balls in Buxton later this year. My dear Mr. Darcy preferred the colour to any other, and I must admit that I believe that it suits my complexion. To go with it, I have had this long cloak made, trimmed with matching braided silk."

Her mother regarded these confections with a critical eye, and had to concede that the colour and design were very becoming for a young lady with her daughter's dark hair and slim figure.

Having suitably diverted her Mama from her irritable mood, Elizabeth took her down to take tea in the drawing room, where they could hear Georgiana playing on the piano in the music room next door.

"Do you ever use the piano here, Lizzy?"

"No, Mama, although of course I could do so. It is always a pleasure to hear Georgiana play so well, but I have never wished to apply myself frequently enough to achieve that level of competence. As you know, I always prefer to read a book, or go for a walk – and take particular pleasure in those occupations which Mr. Darcy and I can share."

Mrs. Bennet, who had never been known to open a book with any enthusiasm, intended to make a cutting remark about too much reading being unsuitable for a lady, but then recalled that Lizzy was unlikely to agree, since she and her father had always shared their pleasure in that pastime.

As her daughter knew perfectly well that her mother had no interest in books, and was equally disinclined to occupy herself with embroidery or music, it was difficult to devise many other ways of passing the time during her stay. Elizabeth did not share her mother's delight in gossiping about her family and friends. Eventually, she went to speak to Mr. Darcy, to suggest that she might take her dear Mama to the town of Buxton on the following morning, which should occupy most of the daylight hours.

"I hope you will not mind, Elizabeth, if I excuse myself from accompanying you on that interesting expedition. There are several matters that I need to deal with here with my factor concerning the estate. Georgiana and I will look forward to seeing you both return here in time for dinner."

And he gave her a sympathetic smile, full of meaning and mischief, which she returned in good measure.

Mrs. Bennet had no difficulty in maintaining a continuous conversation on the journey to their destination. She had already explained that they would not have time to visit the hot springs in the town, or to take the waters. However, her Mama was much more interested in visiting the shops around the market place than in improving her health.

When Elizabeth reached Buxton with her mother, she sent the coachman to the best inn to make arrangements for a light luncheon in about an hour's time.

"Let us alight from the carriage here, Mama. I have found that there are some very pleasant shops in this town that I am sure you will enjoy. I should like to treat you to a new bonnet, if you will allow me, and perhaps a pelisse or a shawl to match?"

Mrs. Bennet was never averse to such an invitation during a shopping excursion, or to an opportunity to make some new purchases for herself and her younger daughters. So Elizabeth and her mother were able to occupy themselves usefully for some time in several of the establishments close to the market place. They found a delightful pale grey straw bonnet for Mrs. Bennet in the milliners, and an expensive matching shawl in the same shop, just like the one that her friend Lady Lucas had recently acquired in London. In the second establishment that they visited, Elizabeth found various colourful ribbons to send back with Mama to Longbourn as presents for her sisters Mary and Kitty.

"This has been the most delightful excursion, Lizzy," pronounced Mrs. Bennet as they finished their luncheon in the private room at the inn. "The selection of goods in our local town is so much more restricted than here. I do wish that Mr. Bennet would not insist on continuing to live in such a very remote location in Hertfordshire!"

Quite apart from the fact that her parents' home was within easy walking distance of Meryton, Elizabeth could not imagine any circumstances in which her father would be willing to leave his beloved Longbourn, with or without Mrs. Bennet. However, it did not seem a good moment to express that opinion. So she contented herself with collecting up their purchases, and suggesting that they go and find the carriage, ready for the journey back to Pemberley.

After their return, Mrs. Bennet was in such a sunny mood that she was able to converse with Georgiana and her brother during dinner in what she thought was a most ladylike manner, suitable for her particularly elegant surroundings.

In the little time remaining to be occupied, Mrs. Bennet made sure that she inspected the progress in the vegetable plots at the cottages, and checked on the health of the little girl who was under the care of the local doctor.

"I do hope, my dear, that when I have returned home to Longbourn you will not neglect to see how things are going on there. Please send me regular reports, for I should be very displeased if all my efforts have been in vain!"

Darcy, standing on the other side of the room beyond Mrs. Bennet, looked at his wife with an enigmatic expression which, some months ago, she would have been unable to interpret.

However, now Elizabeth knew him well enough not to overlook the amusement in his eyes at this pronouncement, and allowed her mouth to show a little smile, to convey a private message between them.

Georgiana, who was learning to understand some of the subtle exchanges between her brother and her sister-in-law, felt some of the warm glow between them, and resolved even more fervently than before never to marry unless she could find someone who would look at her like that.

It had been agreed that, on the last day of the visit, a distant acquaintance of the Bennet family who lived nearby should be invited to luncheon at Pemberley. This lady had previously lived in Hertfordshire not far from Longbourn, but on being widowed some years earlier had returned to the county of her birth, to be closer to her married daughter and grand-children.

Mrs. Bennet had been keen to renew her contact with Mrs. Trevor, who was a dignified person of advancing years with an aristocratic bearing. Elizabeth had made sure that a suitably elaborate luncheon had been devised to impress her mother's friend, who was most gracious in her appreciation of the trouble taken to entertain her.

Darcy and Georgiana were not present at this repast, as her husband had taken his sister with him on a pre-arranged excursion to see one of her childhood friends, who was recovering from a riding accident.

Elizabeth was very grateful that they were not there when Mrs. Trevor mentioned having met Darcy's aunt, Lady Catherine, on several occasions at Pemberley some years ago, before the death of her younger sister, Mrs. Darcy, the mother of Georgiana and her brother.

At this disclosure, Mrs. Bennet immediately launched a flood of words to describe her personal opinion of Darcy's aunt.

Dialogue with Darcy

"When Lady Catherine de Bourgh came to our house at Longbourn, only a few months ago, I thought that she was far from being a pleasant acquaintance – so haughty and proud! And I have been told that her daughter is very unattractive and .."

"Mama!" Elizabeth intervened before any more damage could be done. "You have only met Lady Catherine once to my knowledge, and then very briefly, and you have never met Miss Anne de Bourgh! I'm sure that Mrs. Trevor does not wish to hear anything at all about your opinion of a person with whom you have so little contact!"

And, rising from her seat at the dining table, she went over to the sideboard and said, "Mrs. Trevor, please let me pass you some more of this chicken dish; it is one of our cook's special recipes."

Mrs. Trevor turned away from listening to Mrs. Bennet, and did as Elizabeth suggested, with a sympathetic smile at her hostess, and the conversation moved on to less contentious matters.

"I understand that your elder daughter, Mrs. Bingley, currently lives near you in Herefordshire, Mrs. Bennet. You will be looking forward to seeing her when you return to Longbourn? Are they planning to stay in that county?"

Unwilling to admit to Mrs. Trevor that she was not privy to their future plans, Mrs. Bennet said that Jane and Mr. Bingley had only been living in the county for a few months since their marriage, but that she looked forward to hearing whether they had any new intentions soon.

"I have hoped that my Jane may be already in the family way," Mrs Bennet confided in Mrs. Trevor. "What delightful news that would be for all of us!"

"Mama, please do not speculate about Jane and what can only be a rumour. It does not seem likely that my sister would want it spread abroad, even if it were to be true."

Mrs. Trevor had by this time got the measure of her fellow guest, and reassured Elizabeth by saying firmly, "Rest assured, Mrs. Darcy, that I will say nothing at all about that subject to anyone until I hear it from your own lips!"

However, although Mrs. Bennet looked decidedly affronted at this set-down, Elizabeth's expression did not encourage her to pursue the matter further, so she changed the subject to that of another of her daughters.

"My youngest girl Lydia was also married last year, Mrs. Trevor, to an acquaintance of Mr. Darcy's, a Mr. Wickham. He has a new commission in his regiment and has been posted to Newcastle. Unfortunately I have not been able to see her since they travelled north after their wedding last July."

If she starts talking about the prospect of Darcy and I having a child, Elizabeth thought, I shall no longer be able to contain my temper. There had been several occasions during the past few days when her Mama had attempted to begin on that subject, but her daughter had managed to steer the conversation in another direction on each occasion.

Fortunately for Elizabeth, Darcy and Georgiana now arrived back from their errand, as her efforts to maintain a lively conversation between the two visitors were beginning to flag. Darcy could tell from his wife's strained expression that it had been a rather tiresome afternoon, and so exerted himself to be particularly pleasant to Mrs. Trevor, including agreeing to pass on some messages to his aunt when he should next see Lady Catherine and Miss Anne de Bourgh.

It had, Elizabeth reported to Mr. Darcy later that evening, certainly been a rather tiring day, and she had to admit that she would be relieved when his carriage had safely deposited her Mama in Derby on the following morning, in time to catch the stage to the South.

He came across the room and stroked her hair softly, before saying, "You cannot be surprised at what occurred today, but entertaining your mother had to be done, and she will only remember what she chooses to recall, so do not fret yourself, my dearest."

His wife appeared rather reluctant to accept the truth of these remarks, so Darcy added, "I would be willing to wager a hundred pounds, without any risk of loss, that not a word of criticism will ever pass her lips once she has returned to Longbourn. We shall be reported as being the most benevolent hosts that ever existed in Derbyshire!"

And finally she was able to laugh with him, and relax from the pressures of the day.

Mrs. Bennet's farewells on the following morning were as effusive as her host had anticipated, and she pressed Darcy, her daughter, and even Georgiana, to hasten south to visit Longbourn as soon as their other responsibilities would allow. They all replied pleasantly enough, but with generalities, since this was not the moment to disclose that they were expecting a visit to Pemberley within the next few weeks from Jane and Mr. Bingley.

"My dears, thank you for all your most generous hospitality," said Mrs. Bennet, leaning out of the carriage window as the wheels began to roll forward and take her away along the drive.

"I must find time soon," said Elizabeth to Georgiana as they walked back into the house, "to write to my father, to give him an accurate account of dear Mama's visit to Pemberley, so that that he can make a comparison with what my mother tells him."

Georgiana looked at her cautiously, and then said, "Although I very much regret my mother's early death, I can see that dealing with one's parents may sometimes be a very difficult

experience. Please be honest with me, Elizabeth.
You did mean it when you told me that there was
no hurry for me to consider matrimony?"

"Of course I did, Georgiana, as long as you
promise when the time comes to select someone
who has a genuine sense of humour, and whose
parent will not spend their whole time telling
either of us what to do!"

Dialogue with Darcy

CHAPTER THREE

After Mrs. Bennet's return to Longbourn, Darcy kept his promise and paid for the doctor to visit his tenant's sick child several times until all signs of the measles' infection had disappeared.

"You will not be surprised to learn," said his wife, looking up from reading the latest missive that had arrived from Hertfordshire, "that Mama is almost disappointed to find that everything has been done as she had asked," and her secret smile flickered across her face.

"Indeed?" he said, trying to keep a severe expression as he replied, but failing miserably.

"But she does have one characteristic in common with you, my dear sir."

"And what is that?" Darcy said cautiously, anticipating correctly that he was about to be teased by Elizabeth.

"That she seems to think that one of her most urgent missions in life is to see your sister married as soon as possible."

"Then perhaps," said a voice from the library doorway, "she has not discovered that I have a mind of my own, and can manage my own affairs," and Georgiana came across the room and sat down next to her sister-in-law.

Not for the first time, Darcy was content to see the two ladies that he loved the most in the world sitting together in harmony, and decided not to rise to the bait.

Instead, he inquired of his wife what other correspondence had arrived for her by the post that morning.

Dialogue with Darcy

"My second letter was from Mrs. Trevor, who you will recall came to visit whilst Mama was staying here at Pemberley. She is anxious to return our hospitality, and asks if I can join her for luncheon at her home in ten days' time."

Turning to Georgiana, she added, "And Mrs. Trevor inquires if you would like to go with me. Although you were here for only a small part of her visit, you will know whether you might like to accept her invitation?"

Georgiana smiled and replied, "I found her very pleasant, and should be glad to join you. Where does she live?"

"About ten miles on the far side of Lambton, I believe, on the road beyond Cressborough Castle towards Derby. I suppose that the journey would take us about forty five minutes in the carriage?"

So it was agreed that Elizabeth should reply to the invitation, and her letter went by the next post.

In the meantime, the engineer Mr. James Fraser paid a return visit to Pemberley to explore making further modifications to the steam engine, to increase the pumping capacity from the river. Darcy invited him to stay for a light meal with the family and, as before, Elizabeth found herself less enthralled by the technicalities being discussed than Georgiana.

The young man took considerable trouble to explain the details to them about what was being proposed for the modification of the engine. Over lunch Elizabeth and Georgiana also heard more about Mr. Fraser's family in Scotland and his time at university.

Elizabeth was beginning to wonder whether it was the steam engine that so interested Georgiana, or that the focus of her attention was James Fraser himself. But bearing in mind her dear Darcy's attitude to his sister's future alliance, Elizabeth decided to keep her thoughts to herself, at least for the moment.

"Does your elder brother live in Scotland, Mr. Fraser?" asked Elizabeth during a lull in the conversation.

"Yes, he does. In the longer term, the idea is that Angus should take over the management of the family's estate in Perthshire from our father."

Elizabeth reflected, not for the first time, that almost everyone's family except her own seemed to have large landed estates, but that did not seem to matter anymore, now that she was married to her dearest Darcy.

He seemed to be satisfied with the outcome of the engineer's visit, and went off with his farm manager to oversee the changes that were being proposed. Georgiana agreed with Elizabeth's suggestion that they should both catch up with their correspondence, and a letter came confirming that they should visit Mrs. Trevor on the following day.

When they had started on that journey, Elizabeth realised that she was not familiar with the route after they had passed through the small town of Lambton. The weather was rather grey, and so the low hills and the fields on either side of the road were not shown to their best advantage. The carriage soon passed through a hamlet, and the Derby Road continued through a larger village. That was close to the entrance to Cressborough Castle, built on a rocky bluff rising high above the adjoining ground, with no apparent entry point. However, their route turned away in the opposite direction and prevented them seeing any more.

"Have you been to that castle, Georgiana?"

"Once only. The Earl and my late father were friends for many years, but since his death my brother has not kept in touch with the family. The Earl and Countess are rather in the style of our aunt Lady Catherine de Bourgh, so Darcy was not anxious to continue the acquaintance."

Dialogue with Darcy

Recalling Lady Catherine's rather imperious manner, Elizabeth could understand why that might be.

"But I was invited to a ball at the Castle a few months ago, to celebrate the thirtieth birthday of the Earl's heir, Dominic Brandon. My brother encouraged me to accept the invitation, so that I could meet more young people who live here in Derbyshire. He was right, for I had a most enjoyable evening, and met many new acquaintances there, including the Earl's niece Miss Emily Brandon."

As she spoke, Georgiana blushed a little.

This caused Elizabeth to continue with her questions. "And was there anyone else that you liked at the ball?"

"Miss Brandon's cousin Freddie, the Earl's younger son, was very pleasant to me, as were several other young gentlemen," Georgiana added hastily. These remarks gave Elizabeth cause to wonder whether Mr. Brandon was the person of whom Georgiana had spoken favourably to her a few weeks ago.

At this point, Georgiana changed the subject to speak of Mrs. Trevor and her having lived for many years near Elizabeth's family in Hertfordshire before returning to Derbyshire after her husband's death.

The carriage continued on its way for about another ten minutes on the Derby Road, and eventually turned sharply into an entrance track in front of a pleasant property of medium size, with well-kept gardens on three sides.

"This is the house, Ma'am," said the coachman to Elizabeth as he opened the door and helped them alight. By the time that they had walked to the entrance portico, an elderly maidservant had opened the door and was inviting them to enter.

Inside, they were taken across a spacious hall and through panelled double mahogany doors into a sitting-room overlooking the rear garden, where their hostess rose from her chair to greet them.

"Mrs. Darcy, Miss Darcy, you are both very welcome. I hope that you had an easy journey from Pemberley."

Then, as she turned to her right, they saw that Mrs. Trevor was not alone in the room, for there were two young ladies of about the same age as Georgiana sitting together on a blue settee.

From her sister-in-law's reaction, Elizabeth could see that she recognized one of them, and the young lady in the pink dress with tumbling golden curls proved to be Miss Emily Brandon, the Earl of Cressborough's niece.

When they had greeted each other, Mrs. Trevor said "But you may not have met Harriet Maitland, Mrs. Darcy, and Miss Darcy. She lives at Banford Hall, about a mile from here, with her father Lewis Maitland."

The young ladies curtsied to each other, and Georgiana was invited to sit down on the settee next to Miss Maitland and Miss Brandon, and the three had soon entered into lively conversation.

Meanwhile, Elizabeth took the chair opposite them and next to Mrs. Trevor, who spoke softly so as not to be overheard.

"Perhaps I should mention, my dear, that Harriet's mother Olivia Maitland was killed in an accident a couple of years ago, so she keeps house now for her father with the help of the housekeeper and the other staff."

"How sad," said Elizabeth, looking across the room at the slim girl with dark ringlets dressed neatly close to her head, "to lose your mother so young. Miss Maitland cannot be more than eighteen years of age now. Does she have any other family besides her father - brothers or sisters?"

"Sadly her only brother was killed in the war against Napoleon in Spain some years ago.

Harriet has two elder sisters, Julia and Sophie, but both are married now and live in other parts of the country."

"That must be quite lonely for her sometimes," said Elizabeth. "I know how much Georgiana misses her mother. Although I may disagree with my own Mama quite often, life would be very strange to me if she were not alive, or able to visit."

Mrs. Trevor gave her a wry smile, no doubt recalling the disagreement between Mrs. Bennet and Elizabeth during her visit to Pemberley a few weeks' ago.

"Yes, I agree. However, everyone who knows her says how well Harriet Maitland is coping with her new responsibilities. She has such a cheerful, calm and practical personality, as well as being a very attractive girl."

"And Miss Brandon?"

"I have known Emily for at least ten years. She moved to live with her uncle and aunt at the castle when she was very young, after both her parents died, and they seem to have enjoyed having a surrogate daughter and a sister to their two sons. No one would describe Emily as practical, but she is a very lively and cheerful companion, and has more friends than I can count!"

Elizabeth thought that Miss Maitland and Miss Brandon seemed to be a good combination, and welcome new friends for Georgiana.

"I am expecting one more guest to arrive before luncheon," said Mrs. Trevor, "Emily's cousin Freddie Brandon. He is home for a few days from serving with his regiment, and I thought that your sister-in-law might like to meet him."

Indeed, thought Elizabeth, you may be right, if my guess about Georgiana's interest in the young man is correct.

She did not have long to wait before the door opened, and the elderly servant announced Mr.

Brandon. He was a broad-shouldered young man of middle height, with thick dark hair and strongly marked brows above deep blue eyes – just the kind of person that Elizabeth thought that many unmarried ladies might find attractive.

On being introduced to the visitors, he was quick to reply, "Mrs. Darcy, how do you do? I am delighted to meet you. Miss Darcy, we met at the ball for my brother - how good to see you again! Harriet, how are you – it must be three months since I last saw you. How is your father's health? Is Sir William still prescribing a successful medicine for him?"

Elizabeth soon decided that that it was very easy to warm to Freddie Brandon's open manner and cheerful style of speaking. Any nervousness that Georgiana may have felt to begin with soon appeared to pass, and she did not exhibit any signs of anxiety in talking to him.

Soon all the young people were joining in a lively conversation about acquaintances who they had in common, and what they had all been doing since they last met. By the time luncheon was served, Mrs. Trevor had clearly concluded that she had arranged a very successful social occasion.

Elizabeth was placed next to her hostess at the dining table and, after they had been served, they continued their conversation.

"How is your mother, Mrs. Darcy? Did she have a safe journey home to Hertfordshire? Are you hoping to see your sister Jane at some time in the next few months, before the weather worsens?"

Mrs. Trevor has a good memory, thought Elizabeth, as she answered, "Yes, Jane and Mr. Bingley have written to say that they may be travelling north quite soon to stay with us at Pemberley, although," and she smiled, "I am not sure that they have told my mother about that."

Dialogue with Darcy

Mrs. Trevor returned her smile and said, "It can be difficult for a mother to realise that her children, once settled, are no longer under her control. When both my daughters were married, a few years ago now, I had to adjust to a new situation myself, and even more so after my husband died, when I decided to return to live in Derbyshire."

Before it was time for Elizabeth and Georgiana to return to Pemberley, firm arrangements had been made for Miss Brandon and Miss Maitland to visit them in a few days' time.

"I'm sorry that I won't be able to join you," said Freddie Brandon when the invitation was extended to him, "but by that time I shall be on my way back to join my regiment. Perhaps there will be another opportunity in the future?"

"Indeed, sir," replied Elizabeth warmly, "please let us know when you will next be at Cressborough Castle, and we should be delighted to see you again. Mrs. Trevor, thank you for your very generous hospitality. I do hope that we shall have the opportunity to see you at Pemberley again quite soon."

During the return journey, Georgiana did not seem to be disposed to make much conversation, and this enabled Elizabeth to consider whether her sister-in-law had indeed exhibited any particular interest in Mr. Brandon. She came to the view that, so far, there was no more than the attraction of a pleasant young man encountered in a social situation.

Freddie Brandon was, Elizabeth understood, the younger son of the Earl, so that he would not inherit the family estate. That in itself was of no importance, since Georgiana would have a generous dowry in the event of her marriage. More doubtful, Elizabeth thought, was the fact that the young man had told her that he intended to make the army his long term career.

Her dear Darcy might not be enthusiastic about that.

"But I am able to report, my dear," she told her husband that night, "that all the young people seemed to be very pleasant, and I do think that we should encourage Georgiana to be friendly with Miss Maitland and Miss Brandon, who are both quite close neighbours in our rather sparsely populated county."

"I agree. That would seem to be an excellent idea and I suggest that you do everything you can to promote my sister's acquaintance with both young ladies."

Meanwhile, the subject of these remarks - Georgiana Darcy - was reflecting on a very pleasant day, a contrast to her rather quiet life at Pemberley with her brother and Elizabeth. She had been pleased to meet Mr. Brandon again, although he had somehow seemed to be of rather less interest to her on this second occasion. However, she said to herself, the prospect of seeing Emily and Harriet again within a few days is something for me to look forward to.

Meanwhile, Darcy's new relationship with his wife was, as he had found, in many ways, more complicated than being a single man. Although he was finding married life a delightful experience, some aspects were far more difficult than dealing with his friends or with any of his relations.

Due to the considerable difference in age between himself and Georgiana, Darcy had little experience of coping with younger ladies. The early death of his mother a few years after Georgiana had been born had meant that her softening influence had been removed when it might have been of most benefit to him.

He was becoming accustomed to being teased regularly if he took life too seriously, and very much enjoyed discussing many features of their life together with his wife.

Dialogue with Darcy

The letters that continued to arrive from Lady Catherine de Bourgh with tedious regularity never failed to make reference to the importance of creating a new generation for the Darcy family. His wife Elizabeth was clearly curious to know about the subjects being included in the letters, and he often took the opportunity to read out some of the choicer comments for her amusement. However, Darcy did not think it wise to pass on Lady Catherine's remarks about the need for them to have a child.

Lady Catherine's letters continued to be abusive of Elizabeth's family in a far from subtle way, and this also he did not pass on to his wife. Darcy suspected that his aunt would love nothing more than to visit Pemberley, if only to be able to criticise his wife's domestic arrangements, but he had no intention of extending that invitation, and so far Lady Catherine had not made the request directly.

But Elizabeth did raise the matter once during the following days, when they were sitting together in the drawing room one evening before it was time to retire to their bedchamber.

"I am rather surprised that your formidable aunt has not already come to Pemberley to make her tour of inspection, and to tell us everything that we are doing is wrong here in Derbyshire! Perhaps your cousin Anne de Bourgh is not well?"

"You mean, I assume, that she is enjoying her usual ill-health?"

Elizabeth looked at him with surprise, as he was not usually so directly critical of his cousin. Clearly there had been something in his aunt's latest letter that had really upset Darcy.

"What do you think is really wrong with her? Her life must be so tiresome and restricted, living in that enormous house with only her mother and the servants for company, and never meeting any young people of her own age."

Dialogue with Darcy

Darcy's expression had softened slightly at his wife's calm tones.

"My cousin Fitzwilliam once told me that Anne had suffered an affliction of the heart ever since her birth. I do know that the best physicians have been consulted, and my aunt has said more than once that there is very little that can be done."

"I suppose that, if Lady Catherine had had other children, she would not spend so much of her time trying to supervise the lives of her nephews and Georgiana?"

Darcy smiled at this diagnosis, and acknowledged that his wife's comments had some basis in fact.

"Perhaps I should be grateful that my mother had a more gracious personality, and that Georgiana and I had a very happy childhood as long as she was alive. I find it very difficult to decide whether my aunt was always so overbearing, or whether she has been pushed into intolerance by the sad disappointment of her daughter's illness."

Elizabeth decided to change the subject, and enquired about her husband's other correspondence.

"Did I see that you have had a letter from Col. Fitzwilliam? I thought that I recognized his handwriting?"

"Yes, you are right, although scrawl might be a more accurate description than handwriting. Considering that my cousin went to Eton College, one of the best schools in England, they did not seem to persuade him there to achieve a hand that any of our family can read!"

Knowing that this was a great exaggeration, Elizabeth decided to let it pass, and instead asked about the news that the letter conveyed.

"He writes to say that he will be coming north and hopes to stay with us for three days next week, on the way to see a friend in Yorkshire. The Earl, his elder brother, and the family in

Essex are all well, and Fitzwilliam is looking forward to seeing you again."

Darcy did not add that the letter also reiterated, although in the most civil tones, that the matter of Georgiana's future partner in life should not be raised between any of them when his cousin arrived.

Elizabeth had her mind on another subject, and exclaimed, "How fortunate! He will be here when Miss Maitland and Miss Brandon are coming to see us. That will be a very pleasant day for your sister."

"Indeed," said Darcy rather drily. "Did you tell me whether either of them is an heiress?"

Elizabeth looked her husband straight in the eye.

"I have no real idea about that, sir. Mrs. Trevor did mention that the Maitland's' estate is entailed after the death of Harriet's father to a distant cousin. I did not ask about Emily Brandon but, from what you have told me, the Cressborough family is very wealthy. Are you matchmaking outside the Darcys now for Col. Fitzwilliam?"

He gave her a rueful smile.

"No, my dearest wife, I am just trying to tease you as effectively as you so often do me!"

It was on this mutually happy note that they both decided that this would be an appropriate time for them to retire for the night. Georgiana, hearing them laughing together as they came up the staircase, smiled to herself, and again resolved never to compromise until she had found herself someone with whom she could share such private moments and such joy.

Col. Fitzwilliam arrived a few days later, having had an uneventful journey to Derbyshire from Essex. He welcomed the news that two young ladies would be visiting Pemberley for luncheon on the following day.

Even Darcy was impressed at the magnificence of the carriage with the

Cressborough coat of arms on the side when Miss Brandon and Miss Maitland arrived, to be welcomed enthusiastically by Georgiana and Elizabeth.

After the introductions had been made to Darcy and Col. Fitzwilliam, his wife led the way into the drawing room for some light refreshments. Darcy sat himself opposite his sister and Miss Brandon, and inquired after the health of her aunt and uncle.

"The Earl and Countess are very well, thank you, sir."

"I believe that you have lived with them at the castle for many years?"

"Yes, and before that I was with my mother in Portsmouth."

Georgiana was surprised and asked, "Why did your mother live on the south coast?"

"My late father, the Earl's younger brother, was a captain in the Royal Navy. So Mama lived in that town to be close by when he returned to this country on leave. After the sad news of his death arrived, in an accident at sea, she stayed in Portsmouth because she was heavily pregnant at the time. But neither my mother nor the baby survived the birth."

"I am very sorry indeed to hear that," said Darcy. "So then you came north to live in Derbyshire?"

"Yes. I shall never forget how very kind the Countess was to me at that time. She insisted on travelling all the way to Portsmouth herself to collect me, instead of sending a nurse or a maidservant as many people would have done. I can still remember her coming into my nursery there, and taking me into her arms, and the smell of her perfume in the carriage as we drove north towards the castle."

Darcy's rather negative view of the Countess was being modified by this dramatic account as she continued.

Dialogue with Darcy

"I have been very happy living at the castle with my aunt and uncle, and Dominic and especially Freddie have been like brothers to me. They are very patient, for the Countess tells me that I have a rather lively personality!"

Darcy did not find this difficult to believe, for Emily Brandon had a very quick and determined way of speaking.

After this conversation, Georgiana and Emily Brandon discovered that they shared an enthusiasm for playing the pianoforte.

"My aunt, the Countess, used to play tunes on the instrument at the castle with me using our four hands when I was younger – have you ever tried that, Miss Darcy?"

Georgiana was intrigued to pursue that idea, and took her new friend off to the music room immediately.

Miss Maitland smiled rather sadly as they left the room, and, when pressed to explain, said "I too enjoy playing the piano, as did my dear Mama. But since her death, my father cannot bear to hear our instrument any more, so I never use it."

"How very unfortunate," replied Darcy, "please do take the opportunity here during your visit if you wish. You will be most welcome to do so. May I ask if you know Miss Brandon well?"

"Yes, quite well. She is rather nearer in age to my elder sisters than to me, but Papa has been friendly with her uncle for many years. At one time it was possible that my sister Julia would marry his heir, Emily's cousin Dominic. But then she met Kit Hatton, and Dominic married Christina in London."

"Where do your sisters live now?" asked Col. Fitzwilliam.

"Julia and Kit live in Dorset, on the Morancourt estate which is several days' travel south from here."

Dialogue with Darcy

"And your other sister? Did I hear that she is now the wife of the Duke of Harford?" asked Darcy.

Harriet smiled at his enquiry.

"Yes, sir, you have a very good memory. They were married last year in Bath, quite soon after he had succeeded to the title on his grandfather's death. They live at Harford Castle, on one of the family estates in Yorkshire. Adam is a distant relative of my father's, and will inherit our property instead of my brother David."

"I know that part of Yorkshire quite well," said Col. Fitzwilliam, "as I have a friend, Robert Harrison, who went to school with me at Eton College. He lives about five miles to the north of the castle, and I shall be visiting him soon."

He hesitated, and then added, "I did hear from Robert that your sister was remarkably resolute in defying some highwaymen when travelling with Adam Harford before their marriage? It seems to have been the talk of the county last year!"

"I did not realise that the incident was so well known, sir, but it is true that Sophie can be very brave in adversity."

"Have you been to Yorkshire yourself, Miss Maitland?"

Harriet's expression changed, and she looked rather wistful.

"No, sir, I have not seen the castle, because we have to be very careful of Papa's health now, and only undertake longer journeys when his physicians agree. The property at Harford sounds very interesting, and I do hope to visit Sophie and Adam there one day. But, for the present, they travel to see us at home in Derbyshire."

After these various references to death and illness, Elizabeth decided that this was the moment to change the subject, and she invited Col. Fitzwilliam to escort Harriet to show her the portrait gallery before luncheon. They could hear the sound of Georgiana and Emily Brandon busy at the pianoforte in the music room as they went up the main staircase to see the Darcy family pictures in the gallery on the first floor.

After they were left alone together in the drawing room, Darcy said to his wife, teasingly, "Are you trying your hand at match-making, Elizabeth?"

She smiled at him and said, quite truthfully, "No, but there is little harm in allowing young people to get to know each other better! Harriet may not have many opportunities to meet new people because of her father's continuing infirmity."

Darcy agreed. "If we can keep Miss Brandon and Fitzwilliam occupied after luncheon, that will give Georgiana an opportunity to get to know Miss Maitland also, and for her to play our pianoforte."

Meanwhile, Col. Fitzwilliam was enjoying his role of guide in the picture gallery and his companion's intelligent questions about the family portraits.

"That is my cousin's father Mr. George Darcy, and the next picture is of Georgiana as a child with her mother, Lady Anne, before her premature death."

Harriet stood before the charming scene of the mother and daughter in the garden at Pemberley, and she seemed lost in thought for a few moments.

"I wish that we had a portrait of my Mama to remember her by," she said, and for a few brief moments Fitzwilliam thought that he could see tears in her eyes. Then Miss Maitland recovered her composure, and they moved on down the length of the gallery.

"Where do you live, Col. Fitzwilliam?"

He smiled rather sadly.

"You could say that I do not really have any settled home since my parents died and then, three years ago, I gave up my commission in the army. My elder brother the Earl lives with his wife and two young sons in the property where we were brought up. That is a large mansion in Essex, and I am welcome there. I can also use the family's town house when I need to be in London."

How difficult, Harriet thought as he continued to speak, not to feel that you have a place to call your own home, and then she remembered that she might herself be in that situation when her dear Papa was no more.

"Darcy, Georgiana and I have a rather formidable widowed aunt, my late father's sister Lady Catherine de Bourgh. Her estate is in Kent, and I am summoned, if you will excuse the expression, to visit her twice a year!"

Harriet did not need to ask, because of the way he made this remark, whether those visits were enjoyable experiences.

"My own widowed aunt, my mother's sister Lucy, is quite a different kind of relative from that. She has no children of her own, so she is very kind to my sisters Julia and Sophie as well as to me. I have always enjoyed staying at her home in Bath. Our family had a very pleasant surprise about a year ago when she remarried, to Harry Douglas, who is the father of my brother-in-law Kit. His home is in Derbyshire, at Norton Place, so we see more now of Aunt Lucy than we used to do. Are you a frequent visitor to Pemberley?"

"Yes, since Darcy and I are quite close in age, we were playmates when we were young. I have been visiting Derbyshire for a long time, and for many years before my aunt Anne and later Mr. George Darcy sadly died. I come here now when I am invited, and sometimes when I am not!"

Harriet looked at him in her calm way, and smiled at him, deciding that he did not seem the kind of gentleman who would intrude where he was not welcome.

"Had you met Mrs. Darcy before the marriage?"

"Yes, once, when Elizabeth was staying with friends in Kent at the same time as Darcy and I were visiting our aunt Lady Catherine and her daughter last year. I find her very agreeable, and she has made my cousin a very happy man since their marriage. I hope to continue to be welcome here."

"I like your cousin Georgiana very much. Perhaps it was because I was sent away to school in Bath that we have not met until now. I should love to hear Miss Darcy play the pianoforte. Emily Brandon is always lively and good fun to be with, but Miss Darcy seems rather quieter and less excitable."

Col. Fitzwilliam considered this.

"Georgiana is just growing out of being a rather shy girl into being a more confident young lady. She can be just as determined as my cousin Darcy when she chooses. Elizabeth has been very good for her - someone who is not too far from her own age and can keep him in order!"

Harriet wondered to what he was referring, but decided that it was better not to ask further. At that moment, a distant gong could be heard, summoning them to luncheon, so they returned down the staircase, and Col. Fitzwilliam guided her towards the dining room.

Harriet found herself seated next to her host, and was somewhat nervous about that to begin with. However, Darcy exerted himself to be pleasant and he soon decided that his initial rather neutral opinion of their guest had been wrong. Miss Maitland, despite her relative youth, had a clear mind as well as a pleasant sense of humour, and asked very sensible questions about his home and the estate. Indeed, he soon discovered that she was taking some responsibility for helping her father run their property because of Mr. Maitland's illness.

Dialogue with Darcy

"We do have a housekeeper, who has been with us for many years, and a farm manager who is competent. You look at me rather strangely, sir, but I would have very little to do if I did not take some active part in the running of the household and the management of the farm."

Darcy had not, until recently, been accustomed to being taken to task in this manner, but only a few months of Elizabeth's company meant that he now took this rebuke in his stride.

"You are quite right, Miss Maitland. My sister has not had to attend to such matters, of course, but I have noticed that she too has some interest and ability in practical affairs when given the opportunity."

Harriet gave him a long look that Darcy could not quite read, and Col. Fitzwilliam from the other side of the table said, "Beware, cousin, Miss Maitland may continue to challenge you if you do not concede!"

Then, thinking that Darcy had had enough to cope with for the moment, he added,

"I have just been discovering during our conversation over luncheon that Miss Brandon is yet another of these lively-thinking ladies who know their own mind. The days of subservient young women seem to be well and truly over!"

Emily Brandon laughed at this description, and assured Elizabeth that she could be meek and mild if she chose. Then she turned to Mr. Darcy.

"That is a most excellent pianoforte in your music room, sir. Georgiana told me that it was a very generous gift from you last year. We have had such an enjoyable time playing together this morning."

This reminded Elizabeth of her conversation earlier in the day with Harriet Maitland and, once the luncheon had been concluded, she encouraged Georgiana to take their other guests back into the drawing room whilst she invited Harriet to view the pianoforte.

"That is indeed a most handsome instrument. Do you mind if I play a short piece?"

Elizabeth willingly indicated her agreement and, after a halting start, Harriet played a short tune by Mozart in a very creditable style.

"Would your father really mind so much if you used your pianoforte occasionally at home?"

Harriet sighed and said, "Perhaps not. One problem is that he does not often go out of the house nowadays, or without me. Otherwise I could play whilst he was elsewhere. I could suggest to Emily that she should ask her uncle, who is such a good friend of my father, to invite him to Cressborough Castle. Papa would enjoy that and, although the Earl and Countess would include me in the invitation, I could make some excuse not to accept."

How complicated life can be, thought Elizabeth, admiring Harriet's determination to please her father and care for him. I hope that I would be as sympathetic in the same situation.

Meanwhile, the lively banter of conversation between Col. Fitzwilliam and Emily Brandon continued in the drawing room, observed with some interest by Georgiana and even more by her brother. By the time Elizabeth and Harriet returned to the drawing room, and the two young ladies were due to leave, Darcy was coming to the conclusion that Fitzwilliam might be smitten by the Earl's attractive niece.

But in that he was wrong. Whilst Col. Fitzwilliam had admired Miss Brandon's irrepressible personality and attractive appearance, it was the calmer and more intriguing character of Harriet Maitland that had made the stronger impression.

Once they had said their farewells to their hosts, taken their seats in the Cressborough family carriage and were on their way home, it was inevitably Emily who inquired of her friend,

"Did you enjoy your day, Harriet?   Col. Fitzwilliam is so very pleasant!"

"Yes, but I understand that he is a younger son with no claims on his family's estates.   He will be looking for a wife with a handsome dowry, so is much more likely to be interested in you rather than me."

Emily would have liked to deny this, but was only too well aware that Harriet's prospects after her father's death would be much more limited than her own.

"But you did enjoy meeting Georgiana and Elizabeth again?"

Harriet agreed that she had, and hoped that both she and Emily might be able to strengthen the acquaintance.

Dialogue with Darcy

CHAPTER FOUR

Col. Fitzwilliam left for Yorkshire the following morning, and arrived late in the day at his friend's home. There, over dinner, he mentioned to Robert Harrison the connection between Harriet Maitland and the new Duchess of Harford.

"I certainly would be interested to get to know the younger sister, Fitzwilliam. As I told you when we spoke of this during your last visit to Yorkshire, everyone has been very intrigued to meet Sophie Harford. Her husband had the reputation before his marriage of being quite difficult and not being on good terms with his grandfather. Whether that was true or not, he and his wife seem to be very happy together so far, and they are already making great changes to the estate."

"Well, I cannot comment about that. Harriet Maitland seems to be a very pleasant, thoughtful and calm person, and very concerned about her father, who has health problems. She told me that it would be difficult for her to visit her sister in Yorkshire for that reason."

Robert smiled.

"I doubt whether anyone who has met her would describe the new duchess as calm. She does seem to be as single minded as her husband, but perhaps that is just as well, as the advanced age of the previous duke meant that the family's estates had been sadly neglected for several years. I am organising a shooting party here later this week, and have invited Adam Harford. If he comes, you can ask him about his wife's family if you wish."

59

Dialogue with Darcy

After a successful morning, Robert Harrison took his party of friends back to the shooting lodge, where the servants had laid out a light repast and warm drinks to chase away the cold weather. Fitzwilliam took the opportunity for a quiet conversation with Adam Harford, whose imposing height and rather serious demeanour were softened somewhat by his quiet smile. He explained his recent acquaintance with Miss Maitland and her friend Emily Brandon.

"Yes, Fitzwilliam, I am aware that Sophie has been trying without success to persuade Harriet to travel to see us. My wife will be very pleased to have direct news of her sister."

The duke told Fitzwilliam that Lewis Maitland could probably be cared for by his servants for a few days in his youngest daughter's absence, but that the family's carriage was not particularly comfortable for a longer journey.

"In any case, my wife is likely to say that she is quite young to travel on her own unescorted, so Harriet really needs someone to accompany her."

Col. Fitzwilliam agreed with this, as the duke continued.

"On a different subject, Fitzwilliam, I heard you talking to Robert earlier today about an engineer who had been installing a steam engine at your cousin Darcy's property. I would be very interested in hearing more about that, for such a machine might be of great use in the coal mines on our family's estate."

Fitzwilliam explained to the duke what he had heard about the possibilities of the steam engine from James Fraser.

"Certainly I would be happy to assist you, and will obtain details of how he can be contacted when I return from Yorkshire to see my cousin Darcy."

Meanwhile, at home in Derbyshire, Elizabeth felt that she was beginning to get the measure of dealing with the domestic staff in the mansion at

Dialogue with Darcy

Pemberley. When she had visited for the first time with her aunt and uncle the previous year, they had been greeted by the butler, and then shown round the house by the housekeeper, Mrs. Reynolds. Although the visitors had seen several gardeners tending the grounds, they had not glimpsed any of the other inside staff.

At home at Longbourn, the Bennet family had a much smaller domestic establishment. Elizabeth and her four sisters had been attended by a single maidservant who helped care for their clothes and dress their hair for special occasions, but who at other times assisted the cook and the housekeeper. Mrs. Bennet had her own maid, but she also helped clean the house, fetch the shopping from the nearby town of Meryton, and generally make herself useful.

So it was with some trepidation during the journey north after her marriage that Elizabeth thought about the challenges of dealing with a very much larger number of inside servants at Pemberley. Darcy had told her that his sister had only recently begun to spend most of her time in Derbyshire, and Elizabeth surmised that Georgiana may have had very little to do with organising the house previously because of her youth.

"Once we have safely arrived at Pemberley," said Darcy, "Mrs. Reynolds will introduce you to everyone, and explain to you exactly what they do. I suggest that you should not been too much of a hurry to take over the management from her. She will welcome having a lady in the house again after so long, but you will have many other things to discover and learn."

Elizabeth was very grateful for these tactful comments, which allayed her fears somewhat before her arrival.

When she had entered the house as the mistress for the first time, it was indeed a very odd sensation. There were at least twenty staff in the hallway, who each acknowledged her by a

61

quick curtsy or small bow. Mrs. Reynolds offered to take Elizabeth upstairs to show her the bed chambers, but Darcy declined the offer on her behalf and took on that role himself.

"The choice must be yours, my dear Elizabeth," he said as they went up the staircase side by side. "There are two principal rooms, one each for the master and the mistress of the house. My parents chose to share one, and my mother used the other as her sitting room."

Elizabeth blushed, and thought that this was a difficult decision to make at such an early stage in their relationship.

"May I ask you what your preference would be?"

"No, I would like you to decide, but you need not say anything more for now. Let me show you both rooms."

By this time, they were walking along a broad corridor on the first floor. Darcy stopped at the second door on the right and, opening it, ushered her into a very spacious chamber, well-furnished and with tall windows overlooking the park and the lake below. There was a large and handsome double bed with rich hangings against one wall of the room, and an open door to a dressing-room beyond. Opposite the foot of the bed was a second door, which revealed another spacious bedroom with a more feminine feel, including a writing desk on one side and two comfortable armchairs.

"Was this your mother, Lady Anne's, room?" asked Elizabeth.

He nodded his head. "My father preferred to leave it as it was, but I should be delighted if you would like to use the room yourself and, in due course, to choose new furnishings or make any other changes that you may prefer."

Darcy added that Mrs. Reynolds thought that Anna, one of the housemaids, was a very intelligent girl, and might be suitable to be his wife's abigail.

Dialogue with Darcy

"I suggest that you meet her soon, but do not make up your mind straight away."

Elizabeth agreed, and later in the day a tall neatly dressed young woman was introduced to her by the housekeeper. Anna seemed to be a cheerful and sensible person with a nice sense of humour, and Elizabeth liked her immediately. She confirmed a few days later that Anna would be her personal maid.

"And do you prefer to have a bedroom of your own," Darcy then said with a warm smile, "or to share mine?"

She went across the room to him and touched his cheek with the back of her hand, a gesture that he was learning to love.

Then she blushed and said, "I should very much prefer to share yours, sir!"

That conversation had been some two months ago now, and Elizabeth had not had any reason to regret her decision. Having the other bedchamber so close as her private sitting room was very convenient. She was at her desk one morning with Darcy looking out of the window beside her when Anna brought in her letters from the post.

Elizabeth recognized the handwriting at once, and broke the seal quickly, for she had been looking forward to hearing from her sister Jane, and hoped that the letter brought news of the Bingleys travelling north to stay with them in Derbyshire.

"I would suspect, from your cheerful expression," said Darcy, "that you are reading good news, my dear?"

"Yes, at last Jane and Charles Bingley will be coming to see us, within the next two weeks. You will be happy about that, I imagine?"

"Yes, indeed. Is there any other news from Hertfordshire?"

"Perhaps. Jane is hoping that she may be with child, and has been postponing her journey on her doctor's advice. However, she says that she has not informed my mother, or indeed my father, about the news. She will wait to do that until she returns to Hertfordshire."

Whilst his wife penned a reply to her sister, Darcy went downstairs to pass on the information of the forthcoming visit to Georgiana.

From time to time, news had come from other friends that an anticipated birth after a long pregnancy had not ended in a happy result but had, as with his mother, had a tragic outcome. Darcy was aware that this was a far from uncommon occurrence, however skilful the doctor or experienced the midwife was in attendance.

The thought of this happening to his dearest Elizabeth hardly bore thinking about and, when some weeks earlier Georgiana had made reference to their mother's early death, Darcy had rounded on her with unusual vehemence.

"Fortunately, you were still in the nursery and too young to remember that dreadful time. I had come home from school for the first day of the summer holidays, and our dear Mama was resting in her chair overlooking the lake that morning. But when I returned from visiting the gamekeeper several hours later, all was chaos and confusion. The physician was here, I was not allowed to see Mama, and our father was pacing up and down in the library, quite distraught at what was happening upstairs."

Georgiana stared at his agitation as her brother related the events of that day.

"The worst part was when suddenly everything went quiet, and the physician sent for Papa to go upstairs. When he came back after about thirty minutes, he called me into the library. There were tears streaming down his face as he explained that the doctor had not been able to deliver the child - and that our dear mother was dead."

Tears were falling down his cheeks now and she went over to him and held him close until

64

Darcy was able to regain his composure. Then he apologised for his weakness.

"But you will know, dear Georgiana, that was one of the most unhappy days of my life, and deprived you of the attention of our dear mother when you were so very young! Papa was never the same person after that day, for theirs had been a very happy marriage. Even now, I really cannot bear thinking about it, or that anything like that could happen to Elizabeth!"

What Darcy did not know was that Georgiana had been discussing that very subject only the previous day with Elizabeth.

"Does it ever worry you, dear sister, to consider the risks of having a child?"

"No, in the sense that there is very little that could be done about it, except to make sure that we obtain the most expert care that is available."

Georgiana was aware that having children had been discussed between her brother and his wife soon after their marriage, and that neither of them wished to delay the opportunity for too long.

"I should love," Elizabeth had told her, "to have several children before I am very much older, and I'm sure that Darcy would make a very proud father. But sometimes these things do not happen when one wishes them to. My Mama seems to think that Jane and Mr. Bingley may be in the family way, so I shall be very happy if my mother is one of the last to know if Darcy and I follow them in that!"

So Georgiana remonstrated with her brother about his pessimistic view, and pointed out that the majority of women produced many children without such a tragic result.

"Surely you will be delighted to see your friend Bingley again soon, and you will have so much news to catch up with when he arrives?"

Darcy agreed that he was looking forward to their visit with considerable anticipation and pleasure.

Dialogue with Darcy

"Mrs. Reynolds has told me, dear brother, that there is a letter from cousin Fitzwilliam waiting for you in the library. I assume that he is still staying with his friend in Yorkshire?"

Darcy agreed, and wasted no time in collecting the letter and opening it. His cousin had been occupied with a few days' shooting on his friend's estate, and was planning to stay a little longer as the weather had been particularly favourable.

"He says, by the way, that he went a few days ago to Harford Castle at the duke's invitation. Do you remember that Miss Maitland said when she was here that her sister Sophie is married to the duke? Fitzwilliam says that the new Duchess is very single minded, and just as strong a personality as her husband, and that she was very glad to have news of her sister having visited us."

"I wonder what his definition of a strong personality is?"

Darcy smiled. "I imagine that perhaps he has in his mind something like a younger Lady Catherine?"

Georgiana demurred at this description, and added that there was no fault in someone knowing their own mind; it was more a question of how they chose to express themselves.

Darcy agreed, and decided to change the subject.

The visit from the Bingleys was to be the first serious test for Elizabeth as the hostess at Pemberley, so she was particularly anxious to make sure that everything went smoothly. Detailed consultations with the housekeeper Mrs. Reynolds had assured her that all the domestic arrangements were under control, and that the guest rooms were ready to receive their occupants.

Georgiana had met Charles and Jane Bingley briefly at Darcy's wedding to Elizabeth, but this was to be her first opportunity to get to know Jane better.

"I am really looking forward to that. I do envy you having several sisters, and especially so near to you in age. You told me that you had been very close to your elder sister before your marriage, Elizabeth?"

"Yes, that is true. Jane and I have always been very good friends. Mary, Kitty and Lydia are only a few years younger, of course, but both Jane and I found that we had much less in common with any of them. Mary has always been very studious as well as interested in playing the pianoforte, and enjoys reading some of the most serious books in our father's library. Kitty and Lydia, I am sorry to say, seem to prefer rather more frivolous pursuits."

When the Bingleys arrived at Pemberley, Jane appeared to be rather fatigued by the journey and her husband was anxious that she should have the opportunity to rest. So Elizabeth escorted her to the guest chamber and asked the maid to pull the curtains to keep out the sunlight, and she left Jane there without troubling her sister with any conversation.

She rejoined Bingley, Darcy and Georgiana in the main drawing room.

"How did your journey go, Charles?" said Darcy.

"Well enough, thank you. We made one overnight stop on the way but, as you may have guessed, Jane looks to be in the family way, and has not been feeling well some of the time."

Elizabeth and Georgiana exchanged looks at this news being confirmed.

"Jane wrote to me that you have not told my parents yet, Mr. Bingley, and I think that is very wise, for Mama will fuss you both from morning to night once she knows the news for sure!"

He grimaced briefly, as though to acknowledge the wisdom of this remark, and Darcy decided to ask a different question.

"Are you planning to renew your lease on the house at Netherfield, Charles?"

"Jane and I have been discussing that between us for some time. I would prefer to return to the North where I was brought up. I suspect that my dear wife would like to live nearer to Elizabeth, and further away from my sisters in London than we do at present. So we had thought that we might view some properties in Derbyshire whilst we are staying with you?"

Elizabeth was more than delighted to hear about this possibility, as was Darcy.

"Have you mentioned that to Mr. and Mrs. Bennet, Bingley?"

He smiled at him ruefully, and acknowledged that neither he nor Jane had thought it wise to discuss the subject until they had firm plans. He did make it clear that both he and his wife had been finding it increasingly wearing to be residing so close to Longbourn after their marriage.

"Our lease at Netherfield is up for renewal in four months' time, so that is why we hope to take the opportunity whilst we are staying with you to see whether there are any properties in the area which might suit us."

"Are you intending to take another lease, or to purchase an estate of your own? asked Darcy.

"At present, we have no preference one way or the other. We could start by taking a lease for a short period, because that would give us more time to find something permanent which is exactly what we are looking for."

Elizabeth went upstairs after an hour to see Jane, who she found was in the process of changing into a different dress before coming down to join the party. She related to her elder sister what Bingley had said. Jane was rather more explicit for someone who was normally quite mild mannered.

"You can have no idea, Elizabeth, how tedious it has become to have Mama arriving at

Dialogue with Darcy

Netherfield, often with very little notice, to check apparently on what both of us are doing in our own home! I am sure she is well-intentioned, and I certainly hope so, but Bingley and I wish to create our own family life uninterrupted by somebody else's prejudices. The only way that we can see to do this is by moving home so that we are much further away from Hertfordshire."

After her mother's recent stay at Pemberley, Elizabeth had every sympathy with her elder sister. There was no way that she could envisage Darcy being willing to live any closer to his mother-in-law than he already did.

"It may be that the Earl of Cressborough could help you if you're willing to take a lease to begin with. His niece, Emily Brandon, came here with a friend recently to visit Georgiana. She mentioned, although only in passing, that two of the properties on his estate will be available soon. I could easily write to her and asked her to make further enquiries on your behalf?"

The two sisters went down together to join Darcy and Bingley in the drawing room, and it was agreed that Elizabeth should pursue this suggestion as soon as possible. Darcy added that, whilst there was nothing suitable on the Pemberley estate, he had other acquaintances in the locality that might be able to assist.

Jane took a seat beside Georgiana near the windows, and took the opportunity to get to know her better. After a while, the two ladies left to go to the music room, so that Georgiana could show Jane her pianoforte.

In their absence, Bingley explained what he had heard from Mrs. Bennet about her recent visit to Darcy and Elizabeth. Apparently she had found everything at Pemberley quite perfect; the mansion was handsome, the furnishings were magnificent, and all the meals had been delightful.

Elizabeth laughed at hearing this enthusiastic account, and exchanged smiles with Darcy, recalling the various problems that had arisen during her mother's recent visit.

The message to Emily Brandon was sent immediately, and the reply came almost by return.

"Emily has spoken to their steward, who told her that there is a house on the east side of the estate which may become available in two months' time. It seems to be in quite good condition, and offers enough space for a small family, but the grounds are small and the house is rather close to the frontage of the Derby Road."

"That does sound like rather a disadvantage," said Jane to her sister. "I believe that I would rather investigate elsewhere and, in many ways, I really would prefer that Mr. Bingley purchases an estate if he can find something that he likes."

The next day, Darcy took Bingley with him on a tour of the county within thirty minutes' drive of Pemberley whilst Elizabeth with Georgiana caught up with all the other news that Jane had brought from Hertfordshire.

She told them that Mary Bennet was still playing the piano rather less than well, when she did not have her nose in a book. Kitty often seemed to be at a loose end now that her youngest sister Lydia was married and away from home. How odd it is, thought Elizabeth, my life at home there seems such a long time ago and yet it is only a few months since Darcy and I were married.

That evening over dinner, Darcy explained that he had taken Bingley towards the end of their outing to Cressborough Castle, where they had spoken to the steward who was in charge of that estate. It seemed that the man was well informed about other properties that were available for sale in Derbyshire, and had suggested that they should visit an acquaintance, the steward responsible for a property to the east of Bakewell, where he had heard that something suitable might be available.

"So," said Bingley, "we plan to go tomorrow to see what we can discover. Now that Jane seems to be rested from the journey to Derbyshire, I hope that she will be able to travel with me."

So Elizabeth and Georgiana had a quiet time on the next day until after luncheon, when Darcy, Bingley and Jane returned after a very satisfactory excursion. Jane was full of enthusiasm for what they had seen.

"The house there is just what I would like to have, with spacious rooms but not too large, with well kept grounds and a very pleasant southerly view. It can't be more than twenty five minutes' drive at the most from Pemberley, I would say."

Bingley appeared to be delighted, and Darcy said quietly to his wife that he thought the property would suit his friend and Jane very well if a contract could be agreed.

Elizabeth was pleased to see how easily her sister Jane and Georgiana were becoming acquainted, almost as though they had known each other all their lives. However, the subject of her elder sister's pregnancy was not a suitable subject for an unmarried young lady of only eighteen years of age, so Elizabeth waited until she had a private opportunity to talk to her sister.

"How have you been keeping, Jane? You are looking better now, and I hope that you have not been having too many problems with morning sickness?"

Jane assured her that so far she had had very few difficulties, although she was not looking forward to the long journey back to Hertfordshire in a few days' time.

"However, it seems that very soon we shall be living quite close to you, Elizabeth. How wonderful that will be, although I must admit I am not looking forward to breaking the news to our mother!"

Dialogue with Darcy

Her sister agreed with this, and counselled that the Bingleys should not give too much notice of their departure from Hertfordshire, since that would limit the time during which Mrs. Bennet could complain about the change.

Jane laughed, and agreed that this subterfuge might be the best way of dealing with the problem.

"I will, however, feel rather more concerned about our father, since he will have had three of his daughters leaving the district within a few months of each other. Although I suspect that he does not regret the fact that Lydia is living a long way away with her husband Wickham, I know that he values my company when I go to Longbourn to visit. When I do, he talks very often about you, dear sister, and his plans for his next visit to Pemberley."

Elizabeth felt very guilty at this news, for she recalled how anxious Mr. Bennet had been about her decision to marry Darcy, and the long distance journey north that was needed for him to travel to Derbyshire.

Seeing her expression, Jane decided to talk of other things, and asked about Georgiana's prospects.

Elizabeth said wearily that, with first her husband and then her mother, the subject had been too popular recently.

"I have no reason to believe that she is seriously interested in anyone at present. Unlike you and me, Georgiana will have a very handsome dowry with the money left in trust for her by Lady Anne Darcy, in addition to anything that her brother might provide. So she may marry anyone she likes. Darcy's main concern will be that any suitor is genuine, and cares for her, and is not just a fortune hunter!"

Jane agreed that Georgiana was very well-situated compared to any of the Bennet sisters and that, at her young age, she had time to spare before making up her mind who to marry.

Dialogue with Darcy

"Kitty has been getting quite irritable with our father, since he regularly teases her about when a suitor will come knocking on the door at Longbourn to ask for her hand! She really is quite a pleasant girl now that Lydia's influence has been removed, but her interests are very limited. As you know, there are not so many eligible young men in our part of Hertfordshire in any case, so we shall have to see what happens."

"Tell me, Lizzy," continued Jane, "how you are finding living here in this grand mansion? Have you become used to having so many staff looking after you? Pemberley is so much larger than Longbourn or any of the other houses that we know."

"Well, perhaps Rosings, the house of Lady Catherine de Bourgh in Kent, runs it close, but I agree Darcy's home is on a different scale. The answer is that everyone has been very helpful and my husband has been so thoughtful. Georgiana too has been kind, and explained some things that I have been too shy to ask anyone else about, such as why some duties are done by the junior maids and others by the butler. But you are right; I have had quite a steep hill to climb."

"And have the local gentry been pleasant to you?"

"Yes, although inevitably many people are quite curious about someone of whom they know very little marrying the owner of one of the largest estates in Derbyshire. However, anyone whose manner even remotely resembles that of Lady Catherine does not appeal to Darcy at all, and that can be quite useful!"

Jane smiled, recalling the one occasion when Darcy's aunt had visited the Bennets' home at Longbourn before Elizabeth had agreed to marry her nephew.

"That, dear Lizzy, was a day that I shall never forget!"

Elizabeth agreed, and the sisters went downstairs together to find Georgiana before it was time for luncheon. Darcy and Bingley came from the library, where they had been looking at documents relating to the house that might be purchased, and the evening was spent in discussing what else needed to be done before the Bingleys travelled south.

With the pleasant prospect of having them living close by very soon, Elizabeth did not have as much difficulty as she had feared in saying goodbye when her sister left to return to Hertfordshire. She did entreat Bingley, in a quiet moment, to take particular care of Jane in her present condition, and he assured his sister-in-law that this would be his highest priority until they met again.

"I should," said Darcy after they had left, "really like to be there when Mrs. Bennet hears that the lease at Netherfield is not to be renewed, and even more when she learns about the purchase in our county!"

Elizabeth looked at her husband and then replied, "No, I believe that both of us are very much safer here."

He looked at her quizzically, so she added, "Mama is certain to decide that the whole idea is entirely our fault, even though both Jane and Bingley seem to have made up their minds about the need for a change of location long before they arrived at Pemberley."

"And your father?"

"That will not be so easy, for he will lack sensible company of any kind once Jane has moved away. Would you mind very much if I ask him, quite soon, to come and stay with us again?"

Darcy came across the room and took both her hands in his and pressed them to his lips before saying, "He is a guest who will always be welcome in my home."

Dialogue with Darcy

Col. Fitzwilliam's return to Pemberley was not unexpected, but he arrived with a novel suggestion to make to Darcy and Elizabeth.

"The duke, Adam Harford, is interested in meeting James Fraser to discuss the possibilities of using his steam engine for pumping water in the estate's coal mines."

Fitzwilliam gave Darcy more information about the duke's plans for improving conditions where men and children were toiling in water sometimes up to their waists, with several fatalities every year. Harford's concern for the safety of his miners was very creditable, and his wish to remedy many years of neglect in the underground workings.

"I met his wife Sophie, the new duchess, at the castle. There is little personal resemblance between her and her younger sister. Her grace is of average height, and with auburn curls, whereas Miss Maitland as you know is taller with dark hair. But Sophie Harford is very articulate and easy to talk to."

Fitzwilliam went on to say that the duchess was very keen to persuade her sister Harriet to travel north to see them at the castle. But she had said that Miss Maitland needed both a companion on her journey, and a better form of transport than her family had available at Banford Hall.

"So?" said Darcy with a query in his voice, but a half smile on his face.

His cousin looked at him warily, and then continued to present his proposition.

"I wondered if you would agree to Georgiana travelling in one of your carriages with Miss Maitland, Mr. Fraser and myself, Darcy, so that we could stay at the castle for three or four days. Sophie Harford told me that the domestic staff could care for Mr. Maitland in Derbyshire for that period."

Dialogue with Darcy

Elizabeth thought that this was an excellent idea. Darcy was more cautious but, after a few moments' thought, agreed with his wife.

"Yes, Georgiana might enjoy the opportunity to get to know Harriet Maitland better, and to meet the Harfords. She would probably also welcome seeing something of Yorkshire, don't you agree. Elizabeth?"

"Yes. However, if I were Mr. Maitland, I would not entrust my youngest daughter to travel with people who he has not met. So do you think that Fitzwilliam will need to visit him, my dear, with Georgiana before Mr. Fraser is contacted?"

Darcy immediately agreed with this.

"So may I go and ask her what she thinks about the suggestion?"

He smiled at her in acknowledgement, and Elizabeth went to find her sister-in-law in the music room.

They talked the matter over quietly together, and then agreed that Georgiana should send a note to Harriet, to ask if she could call to see Mr. Maitland with Col. Fitzwilliam in a few days' time. If the outcome of that meeting was favourable, then Darcy would enquire whether and when Mr. Fraser could be available to travel north to meet the duke.

"I suppose," said Elizabeth to Darcy later that evening, as they prepared for bed, "that life here may be quite dull for your sister sometimes. I have not seen Georgiana so delighted about any suggestion for some time, and please do not tell me that is because she would be travelling with Fitzwilliam!"

Her husband looked at her with a wry smile, before putting his arm round her in a close embrace.

"No, my dearest, whatever the reason for her pleasure, I shall not be making that suggestion!"

CHAPTER FIVE

Travelling in comfort in her husband's carriages had reminded Elizabeth of the occasion last year when her father had refused to allow her sister to use the Bennets' equipage. That was because the horses had been needed on the farm at Longbourn. So Jane had had to ride side saddle on the mare in order to reach Netherfield House, where she was to visit Mr. Bingley's sisters, and Jane had caught a very bad cold as a result.

"I wonder," said Elizabeth to Darcy, "whether Georgiana is really aware of the very favourable circumstances in which we live? To all outward appearances the Maitland family also appear to be well situated. Yet the duchess seems to think that their carriage is not suitable to make the journey of less a day to reach Yorkshire."

"That may be so, my darling, but we should remember that, in some parts, the road from Derbyshire is very uneven and there are many hills to be climbed. It is preferable to rely on the judgement of somebody who knows the situation better than we can."

Elizabeth had no difficulty in agreeing with Darcy about that, and in any case Georgiana's forthcoming visit to Banford Hall would confirm whether or not Mr. Maitland wished Harriet to make the journey at all, and by what means.

The other issue that she had raised with her husband, the differences between the elegance of the Darcy's property and the Maitlands' estate, would at the very least be an education for Georgiana, who had so far had very little opportunity to see how others lived, or to reflect upon it.

In some ways Elizabeth might have obtained a rather clearer answer to her questions from Fitzwilliam, who was no stranger to travelling in carriages owned by his family or friends, or by the post. During the journey on the following day from Pemberley to Banford Hall, he raised the subject with his cousin.

"I suppose, Georgiana, that you have never travelled in a public conveyance, or indeed alone in the family carriage? I know that Darcy has always been very careful of your safety and privacy."

She reflected about this for a moment. Life had always seemed very straightforward for her, with someone else responsible for making the decisions on practical matters.

"Yes, that's true; my brother has always been very considerate and kind. I had been thinking recently that I should be more grateful for the comforts that I enjoy just because my family has a large and profitable estate. I have noticed that you are not always so fortunate, although you never complain about it?"

Fitzwilliam smiled as he replied, "My life is not as hard as you suggest, Georgiana, and it was my own decision to leave the army at the end of the war with Napoleon, for I did not fancy living any longer as an officer on half pay."

"Will Mr. Maitland mind if we use my brother's carriage for the journey to Yorkshire?"

Her cousin did not answer her directly in his reply.

"I doubt if the Maitlands are really in trouble financially, but they may choose to put all their resources into farming their estate rather than to buy a new coach. That is a responsible attitude for Lewis Maitland to take, especially as the land is entailed to his cousin and will not benefit any of his daughters after his death, except indirectly through Sophie's marriage to the Duke of Harford."

There were few matters of business with which Georgiana was familiar, but it was through Lady Catherine de Bourgh that she was knowledgeable about the consequences of an estate being entailed through the male line.

"Our aunt was vociferous in explaining to me on one occasion about the fact that, when she died, our cousin Anne would not inherit the mansion or any part of the land at Rosings, but would see it pass to a distant relative who refused to have anything to do with Lady Catherine or her daughter."

Fitzwilliam nodded his head in agreement.

"The other issue, I suppose, is whether there is enough money for daughters to have a good dowry when they marry. I am fortunate in that respect, but the same may not apply to Harriet Maitland."

By this time, they were within a few minutes of arriving at Banford Hall.

There Fitzwilliam found a pleasant low built house in spacious gardens, apparently well-tended. The door was opened by a middle-aged woman who introduced herself as the housekeeper, Mrs. Andrews. She led them across the hall and into the drawing room, where they found Lewis Maitland sitting in a comfortable armchair, a rug tucked around him, and his daughter Harriet rising from her seat to greet them.

"Georgiana, Col. Fitzwilliam, you are both very welcome! May I introduce my father to you? Papa, this is Miss Darcy and here is her cousin, Col. Fitzwilliam."

The visitors were invited to sit down on the settee, and a young maidservant soon entered the room to offer some light refreshments. This gave Fitzwilliam the opportunity to observe his host more carefully. Although Lewis Maitland was sitting down, Fitzwilliam could see that he was a tall man but quite painfully thin for his height, with a pale complexion that one would expect in someone who had a serious heart condition.

"I understand, Miss Darcy," said Harriet, "that your cousin met my sister Sophie during his recent visit to Yorkshire? He is particularly kind in offering to assist Adam Harford by introducing Mr. Fraser to him. How is Mrs. Darcy keeping? I think of her quite often, and that pleasant visit that Emily and I made to Pemberley a while ago."

Georgiana assured her that Mrs. Darcy was very well, and told her what she knew about Fitzwilliam's travels, and more particularly outlined his proposal that Harriet should travel with them in Darcy's carriage to Harford Castle if Mr. Fraser was available.

Lewis Maitland, who had been listening to the last part of their conversation, remarked, "I rather suspect that Harriet is more concerned about leaving me here without her, whereas Sophie has a very low opinion of the age of our carriage! It is not as ancient as she might like to suggest, but certainly Darcy's superior equipage would enable my daughter to travel in much greater comfort."

"Papa, you are too unkind, but it is true that I do wonder if you would be as careful of your health if I am away from home for a few days? Mrs. Andrews is very capable, but I doubt whether you would take as much notice of her as you do of my advice."

"I seem to recall," said Lewis Maitland, "that Julia, my eldest daughter, would be perfectly confident that nothing very dreadful could happen if Harriet takes a few days' break from looking after me for the little excursion that is being suggested. I am following the regime prescribed by Sir William Knighton to the letter, and there really is very little more that can be done."

Dialogue with Darcy

Harriet looked as though she might like to disagree with this statement, but Georgiana decided that this would be an appropriate moment for her to intervene.

"I must rely, sir, on what you say about your health, but I certainly would be very delighted if your daughter can come with us. I would love to see something of Yorkshire. Not only would she be company for me, but I would be embarrassed to make the visit to Harford Castle on my own, not having met either the duke or the duchess previously. I can assure you that my cousin Fitzwilliam will ensure our safety, as well as being well able to discuss technical subjects with Mr. Fraser and the duke, should that be necessary."

Fitzwilliam demurred at this particular description of his talents, but was able to endorse Georgiana's enthusiasm for the proposal, and that his cousin Darcy was very happy to agree that one of his most comfortable carriages could be the means of transport.

Harriet turned to her father, and was ready to ask him a question, but he forestalled her.

"Having met Miss Darcy previously, and now Col. Fitzwilliam, my dear, I am very happy to agree that you should accompany them to Yorkshire in order to visit Sophie and Adam Harford. I'm sure that I can rely on your companions to keep you safe throughout the journey and return to me having enjoyed yourself."

Harriet embraced Lewis Maitland, and turned to smile at both of their visitors.

Fitzwilliam encouraged Georgiana to say that they would be in touch very soon to confirm the details of the arrangements, once he and Darcy had been able to discuss with Mr. Fraser when it would be convenient for him to travel north.

On their return to Pemberley, the two cousins went to find Darcy in the library.

Dialogue with Darcy

He was amused at the considerable enthusiasm displayed by his sister that he should write immediately to Mr. Fraser, but agreed to do so later that afternoon.

"Well, my dear Georgiana, you must be very pleased with the results of your visit to Banford Hall," said Elizabeth. "I had not thought it likely that Mr. Maitland would refuse to let Harriet travel with you, but even so it was sensible for both of you to go in person to confirm that. On another subject, I have had a letter from my sister Jane today, saying that the contracts have been exchanged for the purchase of their new property here in Derbyshire, but she has yet to tell our parents."

Georgiana hesitated, and then decided not to ask the obvious question about what would happen when the Bingleys revealed their plans. Her brief acquaintance with Mrs. Bennet did not encourage her to believe that any explanation would be acceptable. Georgiana could only hope that, when she acquired a mother-in-law, the lady would prove to have a more amenable personality.

The reply from Mr. Fraser to Darcy came a few days later. He could be available to travel at the end of the month from Derbyshire to Harford Castle, and would arrive at Pemberley ready to do so.

Georgiana penned a note to Harriet Maitland, suggesting that she should travel to Pemberley a day in advance so that they could make an early start for the journey to Yorkshire. Georgiana also began to make plans about what she might need to take with her to wear, for Harriet had already told her that the duchess was planning to hold a ball for her sister during their stay in Yorkshire.

"I must admit," said Elizabeth to Darcy, "that I had not expected that a short stay for Georgiana away from home would need so much planning!"

Dialogue with Darcy

Darcy smiled, and replied calmly that it mattered not how much planning would be required as long as his sister enjoyed herself. He added that he thought that Fitzwilliam would not have the same problems, since he was much more accustomed to staying in other people's houses and going to balls!

Col. Fitzwilliam would not have agreed with this description of his social life being so grand, but he was happy to go along with Georgiana's excitement about the forthcoming trip.

Elizabeth had noticed that her sister-in-law had been taking more interest than before in the way that the steam engine on Darcy's estate was being employed, and correctly surmised that Georgiana was anxious to make a good impression when Mr. Fraser arrived, and travelled with her to Yorkshire. Elizabeth was not sure whether her husband had noticed this, and decided not to ask him, for it could provoke him to tease his sister when this might not be wise.

Fitzwilliam, however, had noticed and took the opportunity to ask his cousin what she had learnt.

"That the apparatus seems to work very well, I understand, but that it can be dangerous if not operated correctly. So you may be sure that I have no intention whatsoever of getting too close!"

"That would not seem very likely, Georgiana, and I am sure that Darcy would not let you go to Yorkshire with us if there were to be any suggestion of that."

The reply from Harriet Maitland duly came, saying that she could travel to Pemberley in her father's coach a day before they left for Harford. Darcy saw no problems with that proposal, and Elizabeth was about to agree with him when she happened to catch Fitzwilliam's eye. Whatever the reason, the message was clear that he had a different view on the matter.

Dialogue with Darcy

"What do you think about that, sir?"

"I suggest that I go and collect Miss Maitland in one of Darcy's carriages. As you know, I have no particular occupation at present here."

Darcy could have queried this proposal but looking at the expression on his wife's face changed his mind, for she clearly thought that his cousin needed to be given something to do.

"Very well, Fitzwilliam, as you wish. No doubt you will be offered luncheon at Banford Hall before you make the return journey with Miss Maitland."

Darcy's surmise was correct, and on his arrival Col. Fitzwilliam was persuaded by Mr. Maitland to join them for a light repast. The opportunity to get to know his host better confirmed Fitzwilliam's view that Lewis Maitland had a pleasant dry sense of humour and an excellent relationship with his youngest daughter.

"Do you have any sisters, Col. Fitzwilliam? You may already have noticed that Harriet does her very best to keep me in order, and her two elder sisters are no better!"

Fitzwilliam smiled.

"No, regrettably, I do not have that pleasure. I have only an elder brother, who inherited our father's title. My cousin Georgiana is the nearest that I have to a sister and, although she and I have a very happy relationship, it cannot be the same. I can regularly observe from the lively interaction between Georgiana and my cousin Darcy what I have been missing!"

Harriet had been listening with an inscrutable expression to these remarks, so he turned to her.

"You are saying very little, Miss Maitland, so perhaps you disagree?"

"No," she said slowly, "or at least only partly. It always seems to me that personalities are as important as family structure. My sister would not mind my saying that Sophie was always the most rebellious of the three of us."

Dialogue with Darcy

She looked sideways at Lewis Maitland as she spoke, who nodded his head in agreement at this.

"If you had asked me some years' ago, I would never have believed that Sophie could be happily married to someone as determined as herself. Yet that is exactly what has happened. Adam Harford can be just as single-minded as my sister, don't you agree, Papa?"

"Yes, my dear, that's quite right. I have known of him for many years as a distant relative, since he was a small child. Adam has always been perfectly civil to me, but never appeared to be very content with anything in life before he met Sophie. Now, they each seem to have found in the other what they needed to resolve their own problems and form a strong partnership. But, Col Fitzwilliam, do not let Harriet try to mislead you about herself!"

Fitzwilliam looked at him in surprise, but then saw that his host had a smile creeping onto each corner of his mouth.

"Papa!" Harriet protested.

"By which I mean that my youngest daughter may not be a rebel, but she does very much know her own mind!"

"What perhaps I really need to know, Mr. Maitland, is whether she is capable of dealing with a highwayman during our journey north, as I understand that her sister did last year?"

As soon as Fitzwilliam had made this remark in a jocular tone of voice, he could see that he had made a mistake. It was obvious that Lewis Maitland did not know anything about the incident with the highwaymen, and his daughter had an expression on her face that clearly implored him to say no more about it.

So Fitzwilliam swiftly changed the subject of their conversation.

"Forgive me, sir, that is not a subject that we should joke about. I understand from my cousin Darcy that you and your farm manager here at

Banford Hall may have been using the agricultural expertise developed in Norfolk by Mr. Coke at Holkham?"

His host's worried expression swiftly changed to enthusiasm, and he replied eagerly.

"Our farm manager went to Norfolk at my son's suggestion, before David was killed in Spain in the war against the French ..."

Lewis Maitland faltered for a moment before continuing.

"I am very pleased about the changes to the farm that our manager has made since his visit, to learn about the best crop strains and changes to the types of stock that we should use. As it turned out, the opportunity to make quite simple alterations to the way our land is being used has meant that the size of the crops from my estate have increased for every year since then. That has been most useful at a time when my income from other sources was being reduced after the failure of the bank in Derby several years' ago."

"That is very impressive, sir. My elder brother has more than one farm on the family estates in Essex, but I do not recall him mentioning the systems used by Mr. Coke."

Fitzwilliam was going to continue to explore the subject, but Miss Maitland intervened.

"Papa, the afternoon is passing, and perhaps it is time for Col. Fitzwilliam to take me on the journey back to Pemberley?"

Fitzwilliam could have replied that they had plenty of time in hand, but then he decided that it might be that Miss Maitland was trying to avoid any more subjects being raised that might alarm her father. So whilst Fitzwilliam finished his conversation with Lewis Maitland, his daughter went to ask the housekeeper to fetch her trunk for the coachman to load into the carriage.

They had said farewell to Mr. Maitland and were well on their way through the town of Bakewell before Col. Fitzwilliam apologised.

Dialogue with Darcy

"Please forgive me for referring to the incident with the highwaymen. I had no idea that your father had not been told about that."

Harriet Maitland turned her head from looking out of the window, and looked at him steadily for several moments.

"No, sir, the fault is mine. I could easily have explained that he did not know anything when you mentioned at Pemberley that you had heard the story in Yorkshire. As you may be aware, Papa's health is quite precarious and he might not have agreed that I should travel to Harford Castle if he had good cause to worry about me."

"And do you yourself have any concerns?"

"No, not if I am travelling with you and Mr. Fraser!"

"So you assume that the two of us could overcome any hazard!"

"But of course, sir!"

What was it, Fitzwilliam thought, that he liked about this young lady? She was not the most beautiful girl he had ever met, or perhaps the most accomplished. Yet there was something about her that made him wish that the journey to Pemberley could be longer.

On their arrival, Elizabeth suggested that Georgiana should take charge of their guest, and asked Mrs. Reynolds to show her to her bed chamber.

Mr. Fraser had arrived as promised, and dined with them at Pemberley that evening. He had been very busy since they had last met him, and he explained that the steam engines were being widely employed on estates and in factories in the northern part of England.

"Are you and your colleague finding that there is much competition, Mr. Fraser? You mentioned previously that there were other people who were developing similar engines and products elsewhere?"

Dialogue with Darcy

"That is true, Miss Darcy, but there seems to be enough business for all of us at the present time."

"Has your engine been used in a mining situation previously, sir?" said Elizabeth.

"Yes, there are two in Lancashire that were installed a few months ago, and they seem to be working very well. As you probably know, the ingress of water into the mines is a major problem, and our engines can control that, provided that the quantity to be removed is matched to the capacity of the engines."

As before, Elizabeth found herself less interested in these technicalities than her sister-in-law, who continued the discussion with their visitor whilst she and Darcy conversed with Fitzwilliam and Miss Maitland.

Elizabeth rapidly came to the conclusion that Fitzwilliam would enjoy a private conversation with Miss Maitland without herself or Darcy being involved, so after dinner she made sure that they were seated together in the drawing room, and Mr. Fraser and Georgiana opposite, whilst she and Darcy sat side by side. This manoeuvre did not escape her husband's attention, but he decided to tease her gently to his own advantage.

"My dearest, would I be correct in surmising that you wish to have my company in private?"

Since this was a phrase that he had used previously to suggest some intimate moments, and not in the drawing room, Elizabeth blushed to the roots of her hair, and looked quickly to see if any of their companions were looking at her.

But the two couples were engrossed in their own conversations, so she shifted her gaze back to Darcy's face, and there discovered that not only were his eyes full of affection, but the corners of his mouth were trying to conceal that smile which usually meant that he was teasing her.

Dialogue with Darcy

"Sir!" she protested, but in such a feeble manner that he leant forward and pressed her hands between his and threatened to retain them when she tried to resist.

Fitzwilliam caught the movement out of the corner of his eye and turned but, seeing the intensity of Darcy's expression, just smiled quickly and turned back to Miss Maitland without commenting.

When they had wished their guests a good night and had reached the privacy of their bed chamber, Darcy took her hands again and this time kissed them very passionately before insisting that his wife tell him what her earlier intentions in the drawing room had been.

"Are you trying to put Fitzwilliam together with Harriet Maitland? Or is it that there is already a romance under way there, my darling girl? My cousin needs an alliance with someone with better financial prospects than that young lady, you know!"

She hesitated, rather irritated by his remarks.

"I am not sure what is happening, or that Miss Maitland is interested. I do wish that everyone would not always talk about money in such a situation!"

Darcy continued to hold her hands firmly in his, but this time spoke in a more measured tone.

"Well, we both have reason to know that the unexpected can happen. Fitzwilliam has always been so carefree about matters of the heart, perhaps because of necessity. The more I see of Harriet Maitland, the more capable she seems to be, and no doubt Georgiana will be able to tell us more on their return from Yorkshire."

Elizabeth smiled, realising that her dear husband had no idea that her own interest had been twofold, in enabling Georgiana to get to know Mr. Fraser better.

"Perhaps, sir, we should be turning our own attention to those intimate private moments that you mentioned to me earlier!"

Early the following morning, the travellers' luggage was transferred to the vehicle in which they were to travel. Once they had all settled themselves, they waved goodbye to Darcy and Elizabeth, and the carriage began its journey northwards.

To Fitzwilliam's wry amusement, it was Miss Maitland who raised the subject of her sister Sophie's adventure.

"Georgiana, did your cousin tell you about my sister getting the better of two highwaymen on this journey to Harford Castle early last year. Perhaps you would like to hear that story?"

Mr. Fraser was an attentive listener as Harriet explained how her sister had been travelling with Adam Harford when they had been attacked by the two ruffians. Whilst Adam was fighting was one of them, Sophie was able to knock the other unconscious and eventually the second too was overcome.

"Not many young ladies would be so enterprising," remarked Mr. Fraser.

"No, that was what Adam said at the time, and I agree with him that Sophie is a good person to have on your side in a fight."

"Hopefully," said Georgiana, "we will not have the same problem."

"I at least," said Mr. Fraser, "would be doubtful whether I would be a match for a highwayman, unless I had all of you to assist me."

Mr. Fraser had already noticed during their journey the small differences between the personalities of his two female companions. Miss Maitland and Miss Darcy had seemed to have a very similar approach to life, but the latter seem to be much more interested in his own business. The young engineer was quite flattered by this female attention, and increased his efforts to explain all the technicalities that were required to make a working steam engine.

"I wonder," said his companion, "whether there are any other inventions which will make a great difference in the future?"

He smiled at her, and was happy to enumerate the many new ideas which were coming forward to support industry in the North of England. What he could not realise was that Georgiana had begun to understand that her travelling companion was only happy in describing technical matters. When she attempted to introduce other subjects of interest to her, such as arts or music, or ask him to discuss the recent war with Napoléon, Mr. Fraser was at a loss and unable to help her. So she decided to move on to safer ground.

"I believe, Mr. Fraser, that you told us once before about your family in Scotland. Have your plans changed at all? Does it still seem best for you to continue your career in the North of England?"

He was at pains to assure Georgiana that he had no intention of moving north of the border. This was because, although there were many new enterprises being created in his native land, he had now established so many connections in Yorkshire and other adjoining counties that it was not sensible to have to start again from the beginning.

"Are you looking forward to the challenge of helping the Duke of Harford in the task of draining his coal mines? I know little about the matter, sir, beyond the fact that the ingress of water can be a major problem, which could threaten the livelihood of very many local people working in the mines."

"Yes, that is very true and is a problem common to all kinds of mining, not just for coal. There are many sites which contain valuable minerals but which cannot be worked because of the high levels of the water table within them."

Dialogue with Darcy

Then, perhaps realising that Georgiana's interest in matters technical was beginning to wane, he decided to change the subject. Mr. Fraser had noticed that Miss Maitland had spent quite a lot of the journey in discussion with Col. Fitzwilliam about the health of her father and other matters concerning the management of their family estates.

"Are you familiar with Miss Maitland's family? I understand that she is the younger sister of the Duchess of Harford? Do you yourself have anything to do with the management of the Pemberley estates?"

Georgiana was very surprised at this question, and hasten to assure him that matters of that kind were dealt with by her brother and his estate manager.

"Mr. Darcy seems to have gone to every length to make sure that we travel in comfort and security. Your cousin Fitzwilliam has told me that Mr. Darcy insisted that we should be accompanied by two outriders as well as the coachman on the front of the vehicle and another man behind."

Fitzwilliam had not however told Mr. Fraser that he had thought that so many men were not necessary, but suspected that his cousin wished to impress the duke and his wife when they arrived at the castle.

The travellers took a short break from their journey at a local wayside inn for some light refreshments, but did not stay long, since Harriet was clearly anxious to complete the journey and reach Harford Castle.

When their journey resumed, Georgiana took the seat next to her friend, and Harriet enquired quietly whether she was now an expert on all matters relating to the steam engine. Georgiana laughed, and replied in the negative, admitting that there came a point when one could know too much about such a subject!

Dialogue with Darcy

Meanwhile Fitzwilliam had managed to avoid further discourse with Mr. Fraser about that and, seeing a break in the conversation between his two lady companions, he included them in what he said next.

"When I visited Robert Harrison some weeks ago, his cook fed us all with a formidable array of warming stews and special puddings to keep out the cold weather. I strongly suspect that the cuisine at Harford Castle will be similar!"

"In that case, Miss Maitland and I shall have to ask for very small portions," said Georgiana, "if we are not to return to Derbyshire a rather different shape from when we arrived!"

After about another hour of pleasant light-hearted conversation, Fitzwilliam drew Harriet's attention to a building coming into view in the far distance beyond the carriage window.

"There it is, Miss Maitland, that is Harford Castle."

Harriet turned her head to look, expecting to see a dark forbidding shape set on a hill and dominating the valley below, as she had seem when she visited Emily Brandon at Cressborough Castle. Instead, the view was of a graceful range of pale grey stone buildings, apparently encircled by water, and set in a sunny landscape with a backdrop of trees.

"That looks just as Sophie had described it to me. Although the castle is quite large, I can well imagine that it could also be a home."

Georgiana was not sure that she agreed with this. The property might be more attractive than Cressborough Castle, but she rather preferred the smaller scale and more modern style of Pemberley. However, she corrected herself, that could be said to be a very prejudiced thought, and I daresay that if Harford Castle was my home, I would like it just as well.

As they crossed the drawbridge and the carriage drove into the courtyard of the castle, Harriet remarked, "My sister has told me that the

93

Dialogue with Darcy

style of the building pretends to be much older than it is, so the building has several towers, a drawbridge and all the turrets and arrow slits that a castle at least five hundred years older would have been furnished with."

Fitzwilliam replied that he would not have known that, since the construction had been done with such a skilful attention to detail.

As they all alighted from the carriage and approached the entrance doors to the castle, they were opened by a footman, rapidly followed by an elderly butler who introduced himself as Somerville.

"Please follow me, ladies and gentlemen. Their Graces are expecting you."

The party crossed the hall and went into the drawing room, where Adam and Sophie Harford were waiting to greet them.

Georgiana was immediately struck by the difference in appearance between the two sisters, the duchess being the smaller of the two with a head of auburn curls, whilst Miss Maitland was taller with her dark hair and more sober appearance.

Adam Harford shook hands warmly with Col. Fitzwilliam, and welcomed Mr. Fraser.

"I cannot tell you, gentlemen, how much my wife has been waiting for this moment to see her sister, and we are very obliged to both of you for coming. Miss Darcy, I am especially pleased to have the opportunity to meet you, and very obliged to your brother for offering the use of his carriage."

Georgiana replied that the pleasure was mutual, and that she was looking forward to making his wife's acquaintance.

Later, the duke offered Georgiana, Fitzwilliam and Mr. Fraser a tour of the castle. Harriet preferred to defer that pleasure so that her sister could be her guide. Instead, she and Sophie continued their conversation in the drawing room.

"I must tell you, dear Harriet, about our plans for a ball here in the castle tomorrow evening. Adam and I have invited about thirty local friends to join us for a very pleasant occasion."

"I suppose," said her sister rather shyly, "that I will not know any of them?"

"Perhaps not, but do not let that deter you, for Yorkshire people are very welcoming, as I found myself when I moved to live here. Miss Darcy will be in the same situation, but the duke and I will be very happy to make the introductions. Her cousin Fitzwilliam has visited the area previously, as you will know, so he will have met some of the gentlemen when he was staying nearby with Robert Harrison. I understand that they were at school together at Eton College?"

"I have brought two gowns with me for the occasion," said Harriet. "Perhaps we could look at them so that you can advise me which you consider to be the most becoming?"

Sophie smiled and said, "Perhaps, but I have a little surprise for you. Would you like to come and see that now?"

Intrigued, Harriet needed very little persuasion, but what she found in her sister's bed chamber took her breath away. Laid out on the bed was a fine silk dress in what Harriet knew from the ladies' magazines was the latest style, the colour a pale apricot with a gauze overdress and ribbons on the sleeves. When Sophie held it up against herself, Harriet could see that the gown was too long for the duchess.

"I had it made especially for you. Do try it against yourself for size," Sophie urged and, when Harriet did so, she could see that it was just the right length.

"I hope that you will accept the gown as a small gift from me. I know that you have very few opportunities to go to Derby to the dressmaker."

Dialogue with Darcy

She could have added, but did not, that her sister's pin money would not have allowed her to order anything so fine.

"Oh Sophie, you are so kind! I will be able to imagine that, except for Georgiana of course, I could be the best dressed girl at the ball."

"I'm sure that Miss Darcy has many fine gowns, but she does not seem to me to be someone who would want to outshine you!"

When they returned to the drawing room, Sophie and Harriet found that the duke and his companions had arrived back from their tour of the castle.

"Has Adam explained anything to you about the mines, Mr. Fraser?" asked the duchess during a break in their conversation.

"Yes, a little, your grace, and we shall be going there tomorrow morning."

"I have been told that you would find the conditions for the workmen upsetting," said the duchess quietly to Georgiana and Harriet, "so it is just as well that women are not permitted to do underground."

"But the children are," observed Fitzwilliam. "From what I have heard elsewhere, boys as young as seven are used to haul the wagons to the surface."

Harriet stared at him in horror, as did Georgiana.

"Is that really so, cousin?"

Before he could answer, Sophie intervened.

"That is true at present, but Adam has plans to alter that very soon!"

After dinner, Sophie took Harriet and Georgiana along the wide corridor from the main hall to see the ballroom, a copy of the one at the Assembly Rooms in Bath. She explained that the ballroom had been built for the duke's grandfather, and that Adam had proposed marriage to her there.

"So you will understand that this room is very special to me!"

Dialogue with Darcy

On the following day, Fitzwilliam and Mr. Fraser returned after luncheon from their visit to the mines with Adam Harford. They both reported that it had been a sobering experience, with men and boys working in dark and very wet conditions. The engineer however spoke enthusiastically about the improvements that could be made by installing several steam engines.

"Mr. Fraser has agreed," said the duke, "to stay for another seven days to carry out a full investigation, so he will return to Leeds directly by the post, and not in the carriage with the ladies and Fitzwilliam."

Mr. Fraser nodded his head at this as the duke continued on a different theme.

"Now Harriet, tell me - are you looking forward to this evening? Miss Darcy has told me that she is very fond of music and dancing."

Georgiana blushed at this, and insisted that she had been to very few balls and was not an expert dancer.

"You must be considerably better than me," exclaimed Mr. Fraser, "for all my friends tell me that I appear to have two left feet!"

Fitzwilliam, who was well practiced in the social graces, observed that two left feet could be a serious disadvantage in a ballroom, although he assumed that the engineer was exaggerating somewhat.

"No sir, I am being quite truthful. I have had some expertise in Scottish dancing, but that is very different from the waltz, as well as the quadrille and other similar dances that the English are so fond of these days."

"I daresay," said Georgiana kindly, "that your busy work schedule does not allow you to attend balls very often?"

Mr. Fraser agreed with this sentiment.

When the time came for the ball to begin, the duke and duchess welcomed their friends and acquaintances to the ballroom. Most of those attending were young couples from the local gentry, but there were several unattached young men and ladies who Sophie was quick to introduce to Harriet and Georgiana. As Sophie had forecast, everyone who she met was pleasant and welcoming to the newcomers, and Harriet's anxieties soon began to disappear in her enjoyment of the evening.

Her new gown was much admired, and increased her confidence, since it seemed to Harriet that most of the young ladies were also handsomely dressed.

When the dancing commenced, it soon became clear when he took to the floor that Mr. Fraser had been entirely honest about his dancing skills. Georgiana, who was dancing with her cousin Fitzwilliam as her partner, smiled at Mr. Fraser's attempts to circuit the floor as they moved together across the floor.

"Who are you dancing with next, Georgiana? I saw that your card was almost full."

"That was due to the duchess, who made quite sure that there were very few gaps. I shall sit out the next, and then I shall be dancing with Adam Harford."

However, Georgiana did not sit out the next.

CHAPTER SIX

Miss Darcy was making her way to the other side of the ballroom when Sophie Harford came across the floor, accompanied by a tall broad shouldered young man with wavy fair hair and wearing an immaculate jacket and breeches.

"Georgiana, this gentleman was delayed in arriving and so I have not had the opportunity to introduce him. This is Robert Harrison, known to both your cousin Col. Fitzwilliam and my husband Adam."

The duchess continued the introduction.

"Robert, this is Miss Darcy, who is staying with us at the castle for a few days with my sister Harriet."

Georgiana curtsied to the stranger. Mr. Harrison bowed low over her hand, and then Georgiana found herself being inspected by a pair of lively green eyes in an interesting face.

"Miss Darcy, how do you do? I am delighted to meet you, for I have heard a great deal about you and your brother. Your cousin Fitzwilliam is a very good friend of mine."

Whilst there was a general hubbub of conversation in the room, they both exchanged pleasantries with the duchess. Then, as the musicians began the tune for a waltz, Robert Harrison paused, and then said, "Miss Darcy, is there any chance that you might be available to dance the next with me?"

Georgiana glanced quickly at Sophie, knowing that there was but that one space remaining on her dance card, and then acknowledged that she would be very happy to do so.

Dialogue with Darcy

Once they had taken to the floor, Georgiana soon discovered that Mr. Harrison was an accomplished dancer, and a striking contrast to Mr. Fraser in very many ways. It did not take very long to settle into a regular rhythm and an easy conversation with her partner, and she noticed her cousin Fitzwilliam looking approvingly at them as he and Harriet Maitland passed by.

"I understand that you and your party will be at Harford Castle for three more days, Miss Darcy? I should be very delighted if you were able to spare the time to come and visit us before you return home."

Georgiana wondered who 'us' referred to, but her dancing partner quickly answered her unspoken question.

"Fitzwilliam may not have told you that my mother still lives in our main house. Since my father died, it has suited us both that she should not move across to the Dower House as my grandmother did when she was widowed, but stay for the time being to manage my domestic arrangements."

"Do you have any brothers and sisters living with you, Mr. Harrison?"

"No, unfortunately I have no siblings alive. Fitzwilliam has told me that you and your brother Darcy are good friends?"

Georgiana smiled.

"Yes, that is very true, although there are ten years in age between us. But my cousin will have told you, I am sure, that my brother is newly married to Elizabeth Bennet."

"Has that changed your relationship with your brother?"

"Not in the sense that Elizabeth has come between us. She treats me as another sister."

"Another sister?"

Georgiana explained that Elizabeth already had four sisters of her own, two of them already

100

married and two living with their parents in Hertfordshire.

"I envy both of you in having sisters. I had a younger brother, but unhappily he never enjoyed good health and died when he was less than five years old."

Not for the first time, Georgiana reflected on how fortunate she had been in many ways. Her companion's expression had changed to a more serious face, and she suspected that Fitzwilliam may have told him of the early death of her mother. Whatever the reason, he moved the subject of their conversation back to his suggestion of an outing from the castle.

"I understand from Fitzwilliam that you are very fond of music and playing the pianoforte. If you would enjoy taking a short excursion, I know that my mother would enjoy meeting you, for she was a very fine pianist when she was younger. She is not well enough nowadays to get out very much. Do you think that your friend Miss Maitland would like to come with you?"

Georgiana explained that, as Harriet only had a few days to spend with her sister, the duchess, she might prefer to remain at the castle.

"But I imagine that my cousin Fitzwilliam would be willing to escort me."

"Tell me, Miss Darcy, has your cousin known Miss Maitland long? I have already noticed that they seem to be very much at ease in each other's company."

Georgiana was rather surprised at this remark, and gave the matter her consideration.

"I am not quite sure what you are suggesting," she said slowly.

Mr. Harrison's expression suddenly became rather mischievous, but seeing her confusion he apologised, and explained that he was not matchmaking but only very happy to see his former school friend enjoying himself.

At the end of the dance, Fitzwilliam came across with Harriet to join them, and the couples went together towards the refreshment room. The two young ladies walked together in front, and Georgiana could hear her dancing partner explaining to Fitzwilliam about his suggestion for the following day.

Mr. Harrison brought across a plate of sweetmeats for Georgiana and Harriet, and then began a conversation with Miss Maitland. This gave Fitzwilliam the opportunity to ask his cousin a question.

"I would be happy to take you to Robert's home if you would like to have the outing tomorrow? His mother is now sadly restricted by arthritis, but despite her formidable appearance she does not share any other characteristics with our aunt Lady Catherine!"

Georgiana laughed.

"I am relieved to hear you say so and, provided that our hosts do not mind, I would be happy to go. Mr. Harrison has included Harriet in the invitation, but I suspect that she would prefer to stay with Sophie and her brother-in-law."

Her instincts proved to be right when the proposition was put to Miss Maitland, so Fitzwilliam was Georgiana's sole companion when she travelled the following morning to visit the Harrisons' estate. Once they had left the public road, the carriage traversed a long drive through wooded parkland that in some respects reminded Georgiana of her home at Pemberley. Eventually, they turned a corner and she found herself looking at a property which resembled Harford Castle, although built on a rather smaller scale.

Fitzwilliam could see from her expression that the house was not what she had expected.

"Oh! You do not tell me that Mr. Harrison lived in such state?"

"That would be putting it much too grand, Georgiana," he said, "for the house is a very manageable size once you are inside."

Dialogue with Darcy

His cousin was rather doubtful whether this was an accurate description, but once they had alighted from the carriage and been welcomed by a footman into the main hall, certainly the scale of most of the rooms was rather more domestic than Harford Castle. They were ushered through a dining room with a very high ceiling, with swords and other fighting equipment displayed on the walls, and a very handsome barrel roof. However, Georgiana did not have time to inspect this for more than a few seconds, for their host was approaching and greeted them.

"My mother is looking forward very much to meeting you, Miss Darcy. Please come with me."

They walked on through an anti-chamber with Robert Harrison, and then Georgiana found herself in a much brighter room furnished with handsome mahogany furniture and spacious chairs.

Sitting by the window with the light behind her was a grey-haired woman, her hands resting stiffly on her lap, and trying to turn her head to see the visitors. Fitzwilliam whispered in Georgiana's ear that she should walk up close in front of Mrs. Harrison so that their hostess could see her guests easily.

"Miss Darcy, Mr. Fitzwilliam, it is very kind of you to spare the time to come and visit an old lady when you have so little time in Yorkshire."

"The pleasure is ours, Mrs. Harrison."

Robert Harrison drew up chairs for them both, and his mother continued the conversation.

"My son tells me, Miss Darcy, that you are very fond of music as well as being an excellent dancer!"

Georgiana replied that she was very flattered at this description, although she doubted that it was very accurate.

"Unfortunately, my hands are now so stiff that I cannot use our pianoforte, but I would be very pleased if you could play a short piece for me."

At this point her hostess gestured towards an open doorway on their right, and Georgiana could see a handsome instrument on the far side of what appeared to be a music room.

"Do you have any favourite pieces that I could play for you?" asked Georgiana.

Her hostess enumerated several works by Mozart and other contemporary composers, but then to Georgiana's surprise she added, "But perhaps something different might be best, for Robert can play most of those to me at any time."

Mr. Harrison, who was standing by the window listening to a conversation, immediately observed the surprise on the faces of both his guests. It was Fitzwilliam who spoke first.

"You have never told me that you play the piano, Robert? Is that a skill that you have acquired recently?"

"No, my mother taught me when I was quite young."

Their hostess to intervene to explain that, since she had no daughters and Robert had always seemed to be interested in music, she had encouraged him to develop his skill in playing the pianoforte.

"Perhaps, Mama, Miss Darcy might like to play a piece for four hands with me, as you and I used to do."

Turning to Georgiana, he invited her to go with him into the music room to inspect the choice of scores piled high next to the pianoforte, to see if there was anything that she would be happy to play. Eventually they chose a piece by Joseph Haydn and sat down side by side at the pianoforte.

"I do hope that you know this piece well, sir," Georgiana whispered shyly.

Robert Harrison smiled at her in a reassuring way, and he put the score on the music stand in front of them. Then he began to play the first few notes very slowly. Georgiana, who had been taught to sight read by her London music master, began to join in and soon her confidence increased as she picked up the tune.

"Now let's try a tune by Mozart," said Robert Harrison, and he began to play from one of her favourite sonatas, with his guest soon joining him in the melody. Then they played a short piece by Handel before Georgiana suggested that they ought to return to sit with Mrs. Harrison.

Fitzwilliam, who had followed them to stand in the doorway, was very taken by the success of their collaboration and said so when they had finished.

"All the credit should go to Miss Darcy, for I was already very familiar with the music," Robert Harrison replied.

He led his companions back into the drawing room and motioned for them to take their seats again before he said to his mother, "What you think, Mama?"

"That was so delightful, Miss Darcy," said Mrs. Harrison, "thank you."

Georgiana leant forward from her chair and held the old lady's hands in hers for a moment in a friendly gesture as she thanked their hostess for her kind words.

Behind them, the rather grey sky was being pierced by shafts of sunlight that began to light up the green lawn that extended for some distance beyond the drawing room windows, and something on the grass caught Georgiana's attention.

"Mr. Harrison, what is that on the lawn?"

"Those are hoops for the game of pell-mell, Miss Darcy. Do you play?"

Georgiana thought for a few moments.

"No, but I seem to recall my brother saying that he had played a game of that name in St. James Park in London, not far from the street called Piccadilly?"

Dialogue with Darcy

"Would you like to me to show you what to do? Mama, would you and Fitzwilliam excuse us both for a short while?"

Mrs. Harrison replied in the affirmative, although warning Georgiana that her son could be quite a fierce competitor.

One of the servants was summoned to search for the wooden balls and mallets, and Georgiana and her host then went out into the garden. After observing them for a few minutes, the elderly lady turned to her companion.

"Tell me about your young cousin, Col. Fitzwilliam. She seems to be a most agreeable young lady?"

"She is very much what you see, Mrs. Harrison. Darcy and I are nearly ten years older than my cousin, so it is only in the past year or so that Georgiana has gone out into society, or shared any of our interests. As you heard, she is very fond of music. With her mother long dead, Darcy's marriage to his wife Elizabeth has given Georgiana a lady more of her own age in their household to confide in."

"Does she have many admirers?"

That is an interesting question, thought Fitzwilliam, but perhaps less intriguing than the reason for it being asked.

"She is, as you can see, a very attractive person, but as far as I know there is no one who has interested her. Georgiana has no need to compromise, for she will have a handsome dowry, but her brother is not likely to force a marriage on her against her own preferences."

Mrs. Harrison looked out of the window at Georgiana and Robert Harrison, and then said thoughtfully, "Either Miss Darcy is naturally good at garden games, or Robert is playing rather less well than usual!"

Fitzwilliam, although listening to his hostess, was observing his friend, and was suddenly struck by the expression on Robert Harrison's face as he looked at Georgiana. As he told his cousin Darcy many weeks later, it appeared at the time to be what the French call a 'un coup de foudre' – as though Robert Harrison had been hit by a thunderbolt.

However, Georgiana was unaware of Mr. Harrison's expression or Fitzwilliam's interpretation, and soon it was time for the two cousins to say goodbye to Mrs. Harrison and her son, and return to Harford Castle.

"Will you be staying at Pemberley for any length of time, Fitzwilliam, after you return to Derbyshire?" enquired Robert. "I have some business to transact in London soon, and could break my journey to call in to see you both."

Georgiana's face lit up with a wide smile.

"Oh, Mr. Harrison, that would be delightful, and perhaps you could challenge my brother to a game of pell-mell, if we can find some hoops, balls and mallets!"

Fitzwilliam replied that he had no specific plans to leave Derbyshire for a while, if he would not be outstaying his welcome at Pemberley, so Robert promised to write as soon as he knew when he would be travelling south.

On their return to Harford Castle, Fitzwilliam and Georgiana found that in their absence Harriet Maitland had toured all the buildings with the duchess. Then the sisters had walked together some way up the hill to a viewpoint overlooking the castle on one side, and towards a poor-looking village some distance away on the other, with the coal mines beyond – a very stark contrast between light and dark, as Harriet later described it to Georgiana.

After dressing ready for dinner, Fitzwilliam walked down the main staircase and out into the courtyard in the centre of the castle where, apart from servants going to and fro between the dining room and the kitchens, there was no one to be seen. So he moved on through an archway to the path beside the moat, on the outer side of the castle wall. Having gone some distance, he was about to turn back when he caught sight of Miss Maitland sitting on a stone bench overlooking the water.

"Would I be intruding if I join you?"

She turned her head and, when she saw who was speaking, she smiled at him.

"Of course not, you are very welcome."

"May I sit here?"

"Please do."

After he had sat down on the bench, she said, "Did you both enjoy your visit to see Mr. Harrison? I understand that he has quite a large house and estate."

"Yes, indeed we did, and Georgiana and Mrs. Harrison share a love of music."

"Music can be a great solace."

When she said no more, he decided to ask her a question.

"Would you like to live in a grand property like Harford Castle, as your sister the duchess does?"

She considered this thought for a few moments.

"Sophie presumably likes having so many people to look after everything for her, but I would probably soon find that I regretted having lost the freedom to lead my own kind of life."

"What is your own kind of life, Miss Maitland?"

She laughed, and was about to reply, and then thought better of it. After a pause, Fitzwilliam felt that he must continue the conversation.

"Forgive me if I am being intrusive ..."

"No, the fault is mine. Perhaps I was wondering why you would be interested to know what kind of life I might want."

A direct challenge, thought Fitzwilliam, and I must be very careful what I say if I do not want to lose her.

"I value your opinion. I was brought up in a grand mansion myself, but have never been sorry that my brother inherited our father's title and estates, for there are many disadvantages to being an Earl, or any other member of the peerage."

"For instance?"

"He has very little privacy, and can never be sure whether people are seeking his company because of his title, rather than his own personal qualities."

Harriet replied that she had thought that about her brother-in-law Adam Harford, although he was a highly intelligent man who was well able to distinguish the one from the other.

"So may I ask you again what kind of life you want, Miss Maitland?"

"I suppose to have a comfortable home that I can call my own, shared with someone whose qualities I value."

"Would you believe me if I say that I have only the same aspirations?"

Harriet turned her head and looked out across the moat for what seemed to be a rather long time. When she looked at him again, there was a slight anxiety in her expression, mixed with a quiet determination.

"I would be very happy to know that we share the same opinion."

Fitzwilliam was very tempted to say more, but could feel that they were at a turning point, so decided that it was best for now to move to another subject.

"Are you enjoying your visit to see your sister and Harford Castle?"

Her slightly sombre expression was supplanted by a wide smile.

"Oh yes, although the time seems to be passing far too quickly, and I shall find myself back at Banford Hall very soon."

"Will you mind that?"

Dialogue with Darcy

"Not in the sense that I shall be back with Papa. But I am enjoying meeting new people and seeing more of the country."

Then she asked him what the time was and, having checked his watch, he agreed that they ought to return to the dining room for dinner.

During the meal that night, Mr. Fraser was full of news about his investigations in the coal mines. Harriet, sitting next to the duke, was amused at the myriad details that were being explained to the assembled company.

Adam whispered in her ear, "You will be able to explain all this to my father-in-law when you get back to Banford Hall later this week!"

Harriet pulled a face and replied, "I rather think that Papa will be much more interested in how you are planning to improve the farms on your estate. There is only so much one needs to know on such a technical matter! However, no-one could fault Mr. Fraser's enthusiasm for his subject. Does he have the expertise that you will be needing?"

"Yes, he has, and the sooner we get the work under way the better, for I am determined to improve the conditions for the men and boys working underground. The manufacture of the machinery will take a month or two, for there are other people who are already waiting for their pumps to be made. Then we can install the equipment and start testing to see what happens."

"Sophie told me that she is hoping to start a school for the children in the mining village, so at least they can learn to read and write, even if their families need them to earn some income whilst they are so young?"

"Yes, and I support her in that. None of us around this dinner table can know how hard life can be for some of the people working for the Harford estate."

Harriet suddenly looked much more serious. There might be families, like the Harfords and

110

the Darcys, who were wealthier than the Maitlands, but there were so many more people in England who led very harsh lives and often died as a result.

All too soon the time came for Fitzwilliam to take the two young ladies south, back to Derbyshire, leaving Mr. Fraser busy with the duke, examining the possibilities for using the steam engines in the mines.

Sophie Harford was quite tearful when parting from Harriet, particularly when sending greetings to their father, and in the end Adam had to urge the coachman to be on his way.

Without Mr. Fraser travelling with them, the conversations during the journey back to Derbyshire had a more light-hearted tone than on their way to Yorkshire. Georgiana and Harriet entertained Fitzwilliam with assessments of the skills of their dancing partners at the ball. Eventually they realised that they should ask their travelling companion what was amusing him so much.

"Forgive me," he said, "but I shall never be able to take to the floor at a ball again without fearing that my every manoeuvre is being scrutinised by all the beautiful young ladies who surround me!"

Both Georgiana and Harriet immediately protested that everything they had said was the truth.

"Well, perhaps, and I am willing to concede that Miss Maitland may have charitable intentions. But I know Georgiana well enough to be aware that she might be trying to provoke me! Yes, cousin, you know that's the truth."

Harriet looked rather troubled and decided to venture a remark.

"I am very sorry if I have offended you, sir. You will remember that Mr. Fraser at least was realistic about his own abilities, or lack of them, but there were a few young gentlemen at the ball who had a rather optimistic view of their own skills."

"Perhaps you should venture to say what you thought about mine?"

She blushed, and then looked at Georgiana for support, who encouraged her to continue.

"Do not take my cousin's censure too seriously, Harriet. Since Fitzwilliam has offered you an opportunity, you should take it!"

He thought for a moment that she would not do so, but his relaxed smile encouraged Miss Maitland to speak.

"Well, I can only say that when Col. Fitzwilliam danced with me, I thought that he was a true expert!"

"Oh, do not let that kind remark go to your head, cousin," said Georgiana, "for you cannot rely on every young lady being so charitable!"

Harriet protested at that, but Fitzwilliam assured her that he appreciated her assessment and that having a competent dancing partner was the key to success on the dance floor. That brought a smile back to her face, and he realised how happy that made him.

When they reached Banford Hall, Lewis Maitland had clearly been waiting for them, for he was standing by a window when Harriet led Georgiana and Fitzwilliam through the house on their return.

"You are well, Papa?" said Harriet with a question in her voice.

"Indeed, my dear, Mrs. Andrews has cared for me just as you would have done, and has followed your instructions to the letter. Will you stay for some refreshments, Miss Darcy, Col. Fitzwilliam?"

They both thanked him, but said that they were anxious to get back to Pemberley before dark, and Georgiana and her cousin were just about to leave when Harriet asked them a question.

Dialogue with Darcy

"You mentioned, Col. Fitzwilliam, during our journey back to Derbyshire that Mr. Harrison might be calling in to see you soon at Pemberley. If he were to have time, I should be delighted if you could both bring him across to visit us for luncheon." Then she added hastily, "If that would be acceptable to you, Papa?"

Lewis Maitland enquired who Mr. Harrison was and, on being told that he was a former school friend of Fitzwilliam, gladly supported his daughter's request.

"We are expecting to hear from Robert quite soon, Miss Maitland, and Georgiana or I will keep you informed about his plans. Certainly we would both be delighted to accept your invitation."

Fitzwilliam had previously raised the possibility with Harriet, whilst they had been in Yorkshire, of whether her father was well enough to make a visit to Pemberley, so he thought that it might be worth raising this as an alternative possibility.

"I should like to see Pemberley again, sir, since it is very many years since I was there when Mr. George Darcy was alive. But I would need to consult my physician before answering your question."

Then Georgiana embraced Harriet, and Fitzwilliam bowed to her before they said goodbye to her father and went on their way.

After having delivered Miss Maitland safely back to Banford Hall, the two cousins were glad to be back in the familiar surroundings of Pemberley. They received a very warm welcome from both Elizabeth and Darcy, with many enquiries as to how their journeys had gone, who they had met in Yorkshire, and their impressions of staying at Harford Castle.

"Where is Mr. Fraser?" was the next question, and Fitzwilliam explained that the engineer had stayed on at Harford Castle to complete his investigations at the coal mines. Elizabeth noticed that Georgiana seemed to be quite unconcerned about that change of plan, and concluded that her sister-in-law's personal interest in Mr. Fraser, if any, had been transitory.

"We had a most enjoyable excursion to visit Fitzwilliam's friend Mr. Harrison, and he challenged me to a game of pell-mell on the lawn."

"What is pell-mell?" asked Elizabeth, and Darcy explained.

"And I learned something about my friend that I never knew before," said Fitzwilliam, "even though we first went to school at Eton College together when we were thirteen years' old."

"What was that?" enquired Darcy.

"That Robert Harrison plays the pianoforte, and is quite proficient, or so I judged. Do you agree, Georgiana?"

"Yes, indeed I do, He told us that he has no sisters, and he had been taught by his mother when he was quite young."

Elizabeth was tempted to laugh at Darcy's expression, for it was very rare for gentlemen to admit that they could play a musical instrument. But her husband caught her amusement out of the corner of his eye, and wisely decided to contain his surprise until they should speak in the privacy of their bedchamber.

"Mrs. Harrison was very pleasant to me. Her hands seemed to be sadly crippled. I was invited to play their pianoforte for her – a most beautiful example – although not" (she added hastily) "as fine as the instrument that you gave to me last year, dear brother."

From this, Darcy correctly assumed that Georgiana was speaking of Robert Harrison's mother and not his wife. However, Elizabeth had spoken to him very firmly frequently enough about not teasing his sister when a potential suitor was mentioned, so he held his peace.

Dialogue with Darcy

When the time came for them to retire to their bedchamber that evening, Darcy remembered his wife's amusement at his expense. He was already wearing his night-robe, and was waiting for Elizabeth to change from her day dress, when he sat on the bed and began a conversation.

"I noticed your warning expression earlier. But you must admit, my darling, that there are very few well-educated gentlemen of our acquaintance who can play the pianoforte!"

"But having such a skill is not a crime?"

"Of course not, although ..."

Elizabeth correctly surmised that her husband's hesitation could indicate Darcy's concern that Mr. Harrison might lack some other abilities more common in a well-bred gentleman.

"Your cousin has spoken to us before about his friend's prowess when shooting game on his estate. He once told me that Robert Harrison was Captain of both Rowing and Cricket when they were at school together at Eton College."

"Oh, I did not know that was the case. He seems to be a man of many talents and Fitzwilliam is very fortunate to have such a friend."

"Yes, indeed. Your cousin says that Mr. Harrison is due to travel to London soon on business, and might call in to see us here."

"If he does, I shall be delighted to meet him. Georgiana said very little to me about her visit to the Harrisons' estate, beyond having played the pianoforte for his mother and trying the game of pell-mell for the first time."

He was going to add a remark about Robert Harrison being a possible suitor for his sister, but Elizabeth's quick mind got there first.

"We must remember, my dearest, that neither of us enjoyed having other people trying to arrange our future partners in life, my mother or Lady Catherine for instance. You will recall that Georgiana is no different!"

"But am I not allowed to take an interest in possible suitors for her?"

"Yes, of course. But I suggest that it would be wise not to make that apparent. Georgiana is old enough to know her own mind, and is not someone who will want to be ordered to follow your preferences. We must hope that she has the sense to choose to marry someone of whom we both approve."

And Elizabeth closed the conversation by drawing her night robe around her, crossing the room to sit on the bed beside him, and putting her arm around his waist.

The return of the travellers was followed on the next day by the arrival of two letters by the post, both written in the familiar hand of Lady Catherine de Bourgh. What was surprising was that, whilst one was addressed to Darcy from Kent, the other had been sent to his cousin from London.

Darcy took both letters into the drawing room, handing the second to Fitzwilliam. Opening his own correspondence, he found nothing unusual in the lines penned by his aunt commenting on her normal life at Rosings. But there was suddenly an exclamation from his cousin.

"What is it, Fitzwilliam?"

"Lady Catherine writes from town, having taken my cousin Anne there to see her medical advisers. Apparently there has been a sudden and serious deterioration in her condition."

"I am surprised that our aunt would risk taking Anne that distance, when she would normally summon the physicians to visit our cousin in Kent. She says nothing about Anne's health in her letter to me, which I assume had been written only a few days earlier."

As he was speaking, Elizabeth entered the room and, seeing his expression, asked what was the matter. Fitzwilliam explained what the contents of his letter from Lady Catherine had been.

"Does she not say any more about what had persuaded her to make the journey to London with Anne? May I see your letter?"

Fitzwilliam handed the paper to Elizabeth, who read it swiftly and then turned it corner to corner, for she could see that there was a short postscript along the side.

"Did you see this, Fitzwilliam? She says that Anne is suddenly unable to walk because of severe weakness in her legs, and that the local doctor is unable to offer any new explanation except that it may be linked to a worsening of Ann's heart condition. How dreadful! Lady Catherine must be very worried."

Darcy, who had been listening to this conversation without participating, had never been very interested in his cousin's infirmities, and was inclined not to share his wife's concern. However, he did admire Elizabeth's ability to be sympathetic towards someone who had done everything in her power to prevent their marriage.

Fitzwilliam asked for the letter back, and read the additional words.

"I wonder if I should reply, or wait to hear more? The fact that she has written to me so urgently may indicate that she needs some help."

Darcy was more inclined to think that Lady Catherine had written to his cousin rather than to him because she would get a more sympathetic hearing, and he really could not see what either of them could do at a distance of two hundred miles.

"Let's wait a few days," suggested Elizabeth, "we may hear more from her, or from Fitzwilliam's brother in Essex if she has written there as well. Shall I say anything to Georgiana?"

"No, not for the moment, for my sister has a very kind heart and would only worry when there is nothing practical that she can do. We must await further news."

But Fitzwilliam took a different view from his cousin, and wrote a short note to Lady Catherine in town to offer sympathy and any support that might be of use.

However, when news did come about Anne de Bourgh, it was from a different location and from an unexpected source.

CHAPTER SEVEN

After the various diversions during their visit to Yorkshire, both Georgiana and Fitzwilliam found time at Pemberley passed rather slowly, although for different reasons. As she often did, Georgiana found solace in playing her pianoforte and, remembering the pieces for four hands that she had played with Robert Harrison, she invited Elizabeth one morning to join her at the keyboard.

"You must know, Georgiana, that my skills on the pianoforte are very limited indeed compared to your own!"

However, seeing her sister-in-law's face fall with disappointment at this remark, she relented, provided that a short and simple musical composition was chosen. Needing no more encouragement, Georgiana pulled up a chair for Elizabeth to sit next to her, and slowly began to play Beethoven's Andante in F major.

From the library, Darcy suddenly heard the familiar tune, and then the extra notes being added to the performance by his wife. The memories of an evening at Pemberley a year ago flooded back into his consciousness, and he left his desk and crossed the hall to listen. When Elizabeth lifted her eyes from the keyboard at the end of the piece, she found herself looking directly at her husband, with such an expression of love and longing on his face that it made her heart sing.

To Georgiana, intercepting this, the image of Robert Harrison suddenly came before her, and she found herself examining in her mind how much importance he was to her, so she did not reply immediately when her brother spoke to her.

"You must play together more often," and to his wife, anticipating what Elizabeth was about to say, Darcy added, "I am not concerned about the quality of the performance, my dearest. The pleasure of hearing you both is enough for me."

Georgiana suddenly felt that she was not needed and, excusing herself, she hurried away to her room to examine her feelings for Mr. Harrison more thoroughly in private. However, having spent some time on the matter, she came to no reliable conclusion.

She could remember very clearly the tall young man, and how his fine hands had moved over the keyboard of the pianoforte at his home in Yorkshire. She could recall his voice, clear and well balanced, but never dominant, but what his view of her as a person might be, she had no means of knowing.

"I suppose that I can only wait for the visit that I hope he may make to Pemberley."

Meanwhile, Fitzwilliam had been considering his own position concerning Miss Maitland.

Harriet had promised to write to Georgiana once her father had consulted his physician about making a visit to Pemberley. Fitzwilliam correctly assumed that he himself had more interest in that communication than his cousin, but he did not wish to reveal anything about his increasing attachment to her new friend. He was only too well aware of his own lack of prospects that could compare to those of her two wealthy brothers-in-law, Kit Hatton and the Duke of Harford.

Fitzwilliam was not of a mercenary disposition, in an era when many gentlemen sought to find a wife who possessed a fortune of her own above any attractive personal qualities that a young lady might have. But he was a realist, and he had heard that Miss Maitland would have only a modest dowry and that her home at Banford Hall would pass on her father's death to his distant cousin, the Duke of Harford. Lewis Maitland might not be likely to regard Fitzwilliam as a sound prospect as a suitor, and in any case there was no reason to assume that his daughter had any special regard for someone who she had only met very recently.

Then Fitzwilliam's spirits lifted a little as he recalled their conversation at Harford Castle.

"So may I ask you again what kind of life you want, Miss Maitland?"

"I suppose to have a comfortable home that I can call my own, shared with someone whose qualities I value."

"Would you believe me if I say that I have only the same aspirations?"

Harriet had turned her head and looked out across the moat for what seemed to be a rather long time before replying.

"I would be very happy to know that we share the same opinion."

That did not imply total indifference, and was perhaps as much as Harriet might have felt she could say in the circumstances.

Fitzwilliam resolved, if a visit by the father and daughter to Pemberley could be arranged, to make the most of his opportunity. If not, he must persuade Georgiana to let him go with her to visit Banford Hall before very long.

Meanwhile, Darcy was not aware of anything that was troubling either his sister's mind or that of his cousin Fitzwilliam.

Whilst it had not escaped Elizabeth's attention that Georgiana was quieter and more thoughtful than usual, she at first put this down to her sister-in-law recovering from the exertions of her visit to Yorkshire. However, she noticed that Georgiana was taking more interest than hitherto in the arrival of any letters for Fitzwilliam. Then she overheard her sister-in-law enquiring whether he had received any correspondence from his friend Mr. Harrison, and Elizabeth begin to suspect that a new interest had come into Georgiana's life. She decided that the most she should do was to ask Fitzwilliam, when they would not be overheard, about the visit to Yorkshire, but in a casual fashion so as not to excite his suspicions.

"How was your friend Robert? Georgiana mentioned that you had visited Mr. Harrison and met his mother. You must know them both very well by now."

"Yes, indeed. Robert came to the ball at the castle first, of course. I thought that he partnered Georgiana very competently, and she dances very well herself. Then on another day we both went to visit the Harrisons at home. It is extraordinary that I have known Robert for so long, and yet I had never before discovered that he played the pianoforte. I was tempted to tease him later about that!"

"Why should that skill be so unusual? There are many gentlemen who have composed musical works, after all?"

Fitzwilliam reflected on this for a moment, and then conceded her point, saying that perhaps such skills were better recognised on the Continent than in England.

Despite their continuing the conversation for some time after that, Elizabeth did not learn anything further. She came to the conclusion that either she was imagining something in Georgiana that did not exist, or that Fitzwilliam had not noticed anything, or he did not wish to tell her what he knew about his cousin.

When a letter did come by the post, it was from an unexpected correspondent.

"Whose hand is that, my dear?" enquired Darcy, looking over her shoulder as she sat at her desk breaking the seal and opening the paper.

"The letter is from Charlotte," she replied in a puzzled tone, "I mean Charlotte Collins, and she writes not from the parsonage in Kent, but from her father's home in Hertfordshire, where she is staying with Sir William and Lady Lucas."

Darcy was about to lose interest for, although he wished such a good friend of his wife no harm, her husband the Reverend Collins was far from being one of his favourite people. The cleric was pompous, without a sense of humour, and not capable of making sensible conversation, and his position as Lady Catherine's chaplain was not a recommendation.

But Elizabeth's concerned expression as she read through the letter kept Darcy's attention from straying. When she reached the end of the communication, and had re-read some parts, she looked up at her husband.

"Charlotte Collins has travelled to her parents' home via London. Lady Catherine asked her to accompany them – your aunt and Anne de Bourgh - to town at very short notice when Anne was taken ill, as her daughter's companion was away from Rosings at the time. They went to stay in the Earl's house in Brook Street. Lady Catherine wrote to him, and the Earl and Countess travelled with their children to town to support her, which may explain why Fitzwilliam's letter to his brother in Essex has not been answered."

"Does Mrs. Collins say anything further about Anne's health?"

"Yes. Apparently Lady Catherine visited Sir William Knighton immediately when they had reached town. You may know that Harriet's father Lewis Maitland had consulted him about his heart condition? Anyway, when the Earl reached London, he suggested that a second opinion should be obtained from another physician. I gather that Sir William Knighton was far from happy about that! However, the opinion was exactly the same, that Anne's illness has reached a new and possibly terminal stage."

"Oh, that is very sad news for my aunt," said Darcy, for he was not really a vindictive man despite his lack of sympathy for Lady Catherine in normal circumstances.

"Charlotte goes on to say that, once your cousin the Earl and his family had travelled from Essex, she did not feel that she would be needed for the time being, and Lady Catherine agreed that she could continue on to visit her parents for a few days before returning to town."

Elizabeth could have added, with some accuracy, "and so that she could be away from the company of her husband for a longer time".

"Did Mrs. Collins travel from London to Hertfordshire by the post?" said Darcy, recalling his aunt's remarks during a conversation at Rosings more than a year ago.

"No, the Earl sent Charlotte in his own carriage with the family's coat of arms on the side, which as you may imagine mightily impressed Sir William Lucas when his daughter arrived at Meryton! Your cousin was very kind to be so thoughtful."

Darcy smiled and agreed, and then reminded himself that it was easy, with several carriages of his own, to forget the trials and tribulations of long distance travel for those less fortunate in life.

"Charlotte's letter ends there. Hopefully you will hear more about Anne de Bourgh, either from your aunt or your cousin, quite soon?"

"Yes, indeed. I will go and find Fitzwilliam, for he will want to know the details."

"And Georgiana also?"

Darcy paused and then agreed that she also must now be told what had occurred.

When they went to find them, Georgiana was reading another letter to Fitzwilliam that had arrived from Banford Hall. Rather contrary to their expectations, Lewis Maitland had been told that it would be safe for him to travel to Pemberley for luncheon, if Darcy and his wife would be kind enough to invite him.

Dialogue with Darcy

It was whilst the contents of the letter from Mrs. Collins was being explained to Georgiana and her cousin that Elizabeth realised that Fitzwilliam was much less interested in that correspondence than in the prospect of a visit to Pemberley by Lewis Maitland and his daughter.

Since there was no existing connection that Elizabeth was aware of between Fitzwilliam and Mr. Maitland, another possibility for his interest began to come into her mind.

The cousins agreed that, if a letter did not come soon with more news from town, either Darcy or Fitzwilliam must travel to London to see if they could be of use.

"And in the meantime, may we invite Harriet and Mr. Maitland to visit us soon?" asked Georgiana.

"Of course," said her brother, "for we are all in need of a cheerful diversion. Why don't you suggest luncheon at Pemberley next Friday?"

His sister hastened to write a short note of invitation, and one of the grooms was dispatched with the message to Banford Hall. Georgiana was not the only one to be delighted when he returned with a reply in the affirmative, and the preparations for the visit from her friend distracted her from thoughts of Robert Harrison.

Friday soon came and Fitzwilliam, standing at the back of the entrance hall as they welcomed the visitors, watched Harriet intently as she guided her father to meet Darcy. How welcome and pleasantly familiar was the sight of her calm expression, and careful attention to Lewis Maitland.

Then Harriet caught sight of Fitzwilliam, and they both approached him.

"Miss Maitland, Mr. Maitland, I am very pleased to see you both again."

Harriet looked at Fitzwilliam with her steady gaze as he bowed to her father, and then suddenly a smile spread across her face and she held out her hand to him. He tried to maintain a calm demeanour, and just hoped that she did not detect how much his heart was pounding.

After some preliminary conversation in the drawing room, where light refreshments were served, Darcy invited Mr. Maitland to go with him to the library before luncheon, to examine some volumes that might be of interest to the visitor. Meanwhile, Georgiana took Harriet off to the music room to see some new sheet music that she had ordered from London.

"Sometimes, "said Elizabeth, "I feel as though I'm not needed at all, Fitzwilliam! How about you?"

He was grateful for her humour, but was suddenly aware that, although Miss Maitland might not have noticed anything, Elizabeth knew him rather better. However, he did not expect her to go on to reassure him.

"There have been times in my life, Fitzwilliam, where the end of the world seems to have come, but I have found that one has to be patient, and it is surprising how fate can often contrive a happy solution!"

Fitzwilliam was at a loss about how to reply to these remarks, but she forestalled him.

"Don't say anything if you do not wish to, for you could say that your future happiness is none of my business. But rest assured, Fitzwilliam, that I will help you if I can."

And with that, she pressed his hand in hers, and then went off to see Mrs. Reynolds, to make sure that everything was ready for their repast.

Fitzwilliam had recovered his composure by the time the meal was served, and found that he had been seated opposite Georgiana and next to Miss Maitland, whilst Darcy and Elizabeth gave her father their full attention.

"Have you heard anything from Mr. Harrison recently?" asked Harriet as the next course was served.

Dialogue with Darcy

"No, not yet.   But I'm sure that I will, for Robert is someone who always does what he says he intends to, just like my cousin Darcy!"

"Hmm," said Georgiana, "in my brother that can sometimes be a distinct disadvantage, I've found! However, I daresay that I would dislike it more if he was always changing his mind."

"Some people," said Fitzwilliam to Harriet, "are never satisfied!"

She laughed at this banter between the cousins, and remarked that she sometimes missed her elder sisters being married and no longer at home, until she recalled the regular arguments that she used to have with Sophie when they were younger.

"My father definitely prefers a quieter life, although he misses Mama very much. She was quite a strong character, very like Sophie, so perhaps I am contradicting myself.   Did you know that I am already an aunt, for Julia and Kit have a son who was born late last year?"

"Being an aunt must be a very grave responsibility," said Fitzwilliam, and Harriet looked at him quickly in surprise until she caught the smile in his eyes and was held by his gaze.

Georgiana suddenly had the feeling that she was not needed in this conversation, but Fitzwilliam knew his cousin well enough to pick up her mood, and immediately included her again in a more general discussion with Elizabeth.

At the end of the table, Lewis Maitland was talking to Darcy, and took the opportunity to ask him about Fitzwilliam.

"My daughter seems to have a good opinion of your cousin, sir. I understand that he has given up his commission?"

"Yes, he did not believe that there was a long term future for him as an army officer, now that the war with the French is over.   His elder brother, the Earl, inherited the title of course, as well as the family estates. Fitzwilliam has a modest legacy from his mother, enough to support him, and he is very competent in anything he turns his mind to."

Lewis Maitland looked thoughtful at this reply, but did not say any more. After the meal, Georgiana and her brother took him up to the portrait gallery, where they amused him with tales of their less reputable ancestors in times past. Meanwhile Elizabeth excused herself, leaving Fitzwilliam and Harriet together.

"Would you like to play the pianoforte, Miss Maitland? I'm sure that Georgiana would be happy for you to do so."

Harriet demurred at this, until he added that it would be a great pleasure for him to hear her play.

At this, she blushed, smiled shyly, and then quietly agreed to his request. So it was in the music room that Elizabeth found them when she returned some thirty minutes' later, with Fitzwilliam sitting by the window listening to Harriet at the keyboard. Elizabeth was about to leave them together when the sound of several voices came from a distance, and Darcy and Lewis Maitland came down the staircase with Georgiana and then across the hall.

Elizabeth had asked that tea should be served before it was time for the visitors to return to Banford Hall, so they all moved to the drawing room. Fitzwilliam placed himself next to Lewis Maitland on the settee, and to begin with they both listened to the conversation between Harriet and her hosts on the other side of the room.

"Tell me, Col. Fitzwilliam, you must have served in Spain during the Peninsular War. Were you at Badajoz?"

Fitzwilliam knew what might be coming, for he had heard the story of how Harriet's elder brother David had been killed in that battle.

"No, sir. I had been sent with two other officers back to the coast in Portugal, to collect and train a batch of recruits newly arrived by sea from England. That task had been completed, and we were all making our way through Spain to rejoin the main force. About twenty miles short of Badajoz, we passed a messenger sent with news of the battle."

Fitzwilliam paused in thought for a few moments before continuing.

"He said that about three thousand of our soldiers had died in the fierce battle for Badajoz. It is said that our commander, Wellington, wept at the sight of the bodies of his troops piled high against the breaches that had been made in the walls. When our party reached the town on the following day, we found that around four thousand more people – many of them residents – had been killed by our troops in revenge for the slaughter of their comrades."

Lewis Maitland looked grave.

"I had heard that there was much looting, and worse, after the English and Portuguese soldiers entered the town?"

"Yes, I shall never forget what we saw there on the following day. War can sometimes be justified, but much of what happens during a battle and afterwards can be very ugly."

"I suppose that you might have been amongst the casualties if you had been there?"

"Yes, many men in my regiment died or were injured in the battle at Badajoz. You could say that it is ironic that one reason for my deciding to leave the army was that there is no prospect of more fighting until there is another war!"

His companion smiled wanly, and agreed.

"Col. Fitzwilliam, there is something that I should say to you now in confidence that Harriet has not been told."

"Sir?"

"My physician advised me that I might make this journey today to Pemberley without any extra risk of harm. However, he also explained to me that there is now a slow but steady deterioration in my heart condition and that, one day not too far in the future, I shall have an attack from which I am not likely to recover."

Fitzwilliam was not sure how best to reply to this.

"I would also like you to know that, if you may have any serious intentions towards Harriet, they will have my blessing. You are a fine young man of good character, and you and my daughter seem to me to be well suited. I do not wish you to say anything, for you may not yet be certain in your own mind."

So Fitzwilliam kept his peace, although his mind was racing across his recollection of his various meetings with Harriet. Clearly there was something that had caused her father to think that she was not indifferent, since Lewis Maitland was a sympathetic and supportive parent. However, he was quickly diverted from these thoughts by a question from Georgiana.

"I was just reminding Harriet that you are hoping to hear soon from your friend Mr. Harrison in Yorkshire?"

"Yes, indeed, although we may find that any visit he may make to Pemberley on his way to London is relatively brief. But perhaps, my dear cousin, Robert may find the time to play your very handsome pianoforte, with permission of course!"

Lewis Maitland looked very puzzled at the meaning of this remark, but Darcy was not surprised to find that his wife was looking at him with a great deal of amusement, and had the grace to smile back at her, remembering their private conversation on the subject of gentlemen who could play that instrument.

As the guests left for Banford Hall, Fitzwilliam found a quiet moment to say to Lewis Maitland that he was grateful for what he had said in confidence. He then had the pleasure of holding Harriet's hand for just a few seconds as she said goodbye.

Dialogue with Darcy

More domestic matters held the attention of the household for the next two days. Elizabeth decided to choose some new drapes for her sitting room, as Darcy had suggested to her several weeks earlier, and travelled to Buxton for this purpose with the housekeeper Mrs. Reynolds. There were several bolts of cloth in the carriage when they came back to Pemberley and a whole afternoon was spent in holding each up against the windows to compare the effect, and asking her sister-in-law for her advice.

Georgiana, having played through her whole repertoire of favourite pieces on the pianoforte in the music room, was reluctant to repeat them, and persuaded Fitzwilliam to engage in several games of chess. But that always seemed to end with the same outcome.

"However hard I try, cousin, you are always able to defeat me. Why can't I profit from my previous experience and win at least once?"

Fitzwilliam, feeling benevolent, replied, "I have always suspected that people who are very proficient at chess must have the killer instinct, and sometimes a less attractive personality. In short, you are not evil enough to win!"

This made her laugh.

"Where does that leave my brother, for he can beat me easily at chess whenever he chooses?"

"Perhaps, but I have also seen him lose at our club in town, so he succeeds only when the opposition has less experience, like yourself."

After that, Georgiana and Elizabeth took a walk around the lake in the afternoon sunshine, pausing in all of their favourite places to admire the view. When they returned, Darcy was with his bailiff, who was asking him to inspect the pumping machine down by the river.

Georgiana, with little else to occupy her, went with them and was the first to notice that weed from the water was clogging one of the inlets. Her cousin, on having this reported to him when she returned to the house, suggested that she might have a promising future as an engineer like Mr. Fraser!

"Perhaps we should ask him to come and inspect the pump?" added Fitzwilliam as Elizabeth arrived to find out what had happened.

"I doubt that such a short-term problem makes that necessary," was Georgiana's calm reply.

This answer made her sister-in-law wonder if Mr. Fraser's attraction had been merely that he had brought a novel subject into Georgiana's rather predictable life, and her sister-in-law's reply made Elizabeth certain that any attachment to that gentleman must have been at most fleeting, and had now disappeared from sight.

When the long-awaited letter from Mr. Harrison finally came, Fitzwilliam announced that his friend Robert was indeed about to leave Yorkshire and coming to visit them, and that he would like to stay for two nights at Pemberley if that would be acceptable to his hosts. Darcy was happy to agree straight away, but Elizabeth was almost too engrossed in correspondence of her own to answer, for the letter she was reading had been written by her father.

"Bingley and Jane have finally told Mama that they will be moving soon to live in Derbyshire. Poor Papa, he has retreated from her agitation and all her complaints to his study, and begs to know if you would agree to him paying us a visit here in about three weeks' time!"

Darcy sympathised very much with Mr. Bennet's desire for a quiet life.

"How will he travel?"

"He is minded to come north with Bingley and my sister when they leave Hertfordshire."

"And his return?"

Elizabeth thought for a moment, and then said that perhaps she could travel with her father in her husband's carriage to stay for a few days at her parents' home at Longbourn.

"I have not been there since we married, and perhaps now is a good time to plan a short visit?"

"Do you wish me to accompany you, my dear?" said Darcy.

"You are very kind, sir, but perhaps it will be rather better for me to hear my mother's news in private!"

Darcy was grateful for this deliverance, for Mr. Bennet's letter confirmed that staying at Longbourn at present might not be a very peaceful occupation. Darcy went on to enquire whether Elizabeth's father had conveyed any news about Mrs. Collins.

"Oh, yes! Forgive me for not telling you immediately. Charlotte stayed for three days in Meryton with her parents Sir William and Lady Lucas, and then returned by the post back to town. But there has been no news since then, beyond the fact that she had arrived safely back at your cousin's house in Brook Street to join Lady Catherine."

What neither of them had noticed was that Fitzwilliam had received a second letter as well as the one from Robert Harrison, and had left the room to read it quietly in the library. When he returned, followed by Georgiana, the expression on his face was grave.

"There is news at last from Lady Catherine, who writes from Kent. Our aunt has gone back to Rosings, for the visits to the doctors had been completed and Anne had found the heat and dust in town too fatiguing. Lady Catherine says that her daughter is now able to walk only a very short distance before she gets so short of breath that she cannot continue. The prognosis is said to be terminal within a few months, according to both of the physicians who examined Anne in London."

"And what does Lady Catherine say about your offer to travel to assist her?"

"She says that my brother and his wife have done all that was required, so she has absolutely no need of my company. She adds that the doctors in town cannot be competent, since they can offer no new remedy for our cousin's health except for her to rest."

Darcy made no further comment, although his expression had hardened on hearing about his aunt's brusque rejection of Fitzwilliam's offer.

Elizabeth was more sympathetic, since she knew how she would feel if her sister-in-law or her own dear Jane was mortally ill.

Georgiana was torn between sharing Elizabeth's opinion, and her own anxiety that Fitzwilliam should reply to the correspondence from Robert Harrison as soon as possible. Elizabeth was aware of that, and persuaded him before anything else was done that the message must be sent that day, if it was to reach his friend before he was due to leave Yorkshire.

Later that evening in their bedchamber, Elizabeth took Darcy to task about his attitude towards his aunt's misfortune.

"I really would be very disappointed, sir, if you took such a firm position about the health of one of my own sisters! Lady Catherine may have very many faults, but to be in imminent danger of losing her only child surely deserves some compassion!"

Her husband was taken aback, not so much at the words she used, but at the ferocity with which they were delivered. His immediate reaction was to fire back a comment at her in the same vein. However, that would have been the way in which the old Darcy would have reacted, and not the happy man that he was now, deeply in love with the lively lady in front of him.

"Your charity does you great credit, my dearest. Perhaps it is because I have known my aunt all my life that I have learned to be so wary! Of course your sentiments are quite proper, but I suppose that we shall both have to agree to disagree? My feelings about Lady Catherine, or

George Wickham for that matter, will never be neutral!"

His mention of Wickham gave Elizabeth pause for thought. She was no more charitable about that brother-in-law than Darcy was, now that she was aware of the history of their relationship since their childhood. His wife Lydia might be her youngest sister, but Elizabeth had rarely felt that she had any interests in common with that empty-headed and flirtatious young lady, and she had few hopes that the marriage with Wickham would prosper in the longer term. So she decided that some form of apology was in order.

"No, it's true that I would not want to see either Wickham or Lydia if I could avoid it, or entertain either of them here at Pemberley. Poor Fitzwilliam, he tried to be so helpful to your aunt, and had his offer thrown back in his face! But if Anne de Bourgh does not survive ..."

"In that case, of course I would travel to Kent for the funeral."

"But if you were not invited?"

Darcy considered this point.

"Lady Catherine is, as you know, a great one for proper behaviour and the preservation of the family's reputation. I am sure that I can guarantee that both Fitzwilliam and I would be summoned immediately to be at that sad occasion. Fortunately for both you and my sister, the presence of ladies at funerals is, as you will be aware, not thought to be appropriate in any circumstances."

"What is the position of the Earl about Lady Catherine and her daughter? I only met him very briefly at our wedding, and had no opportunity for conversation then, or since."

Darcy considered briefly the character of his cousin, who had a rather grand manner reminiscent of his aunt's haughty demeanour.

"Being the head of his family, and having inherited his father's title, perhaps makes him more sympathetic to Lady Catherine and more supportive of her views. I have no problem with that, since he takes the pressures away from Georgiana and myself and, to a lesser extent, our cousin Fitzwilliam. I sometimes think that arguments within families can be very like politics."

Elizabeth was not sure for a moment what he meant by this remark, and said so.

"I mean that I can feel some sympathy with our current Prime Minister, the Earl of Liverpool, in having to reconcile the views of his colleagues in the Tory party, like Wellington, as well as needing to try to resolve all the social problems arising from so many men being out of work after the war with the French."

"I suppose that you would be better to debate such matters with my father, when he travels with Bingley and Jane to stay with us here at Pemberley in a few weeks' time!"

Darcy smiled at his wife fondly, and decided that he had strayed too far from other matters that they could pursue with much more enjoyment in the privacy of their room.

When the time came for Mr. Harrison's much anticipated visit, he arrived to an expectant household who had more than one interest to pursue in conversing with him.

Both Darcy and Elizabeth were intrigued to meet someone of whom they had heard so much from Fitzwilliam. Georgiana, on the other hand, was unsure of the level of her own interest until the visitor arrived, but was rather bowled over by her feelings when she saw him again, and was very anxious not to reveal this.

Mr. Harrison arrived late on a rather wet evening and, weary from travelling, had initially to be coaxed into conversation during dinner. To Darcy, the gentleman seemed to be a typical member of the wealthier classes, knowledgeable about politics and the management of his estate.

Dialogue with Darcy

Elizabeth observed the tall, fair haired young man carefully, for the combination of his traditional background with his interest in music was very unusual, and Georgiana had told her that he was also accomplished at dancing as well as in conversation.

Elizabeth also wanted to see her sister-in-law's reaction to the visitor, for she suspected Georgiana might have more than a passing interest there, and so had seated Robert Harrison next to herself at dinner, but opposite her sister-in-law.

"Georgiana very much enjoyed seeing your house during her visit to Yorkshire, sir. I have never been so far north yet myself, but she described the landscape on your estate as being very handsome."

"That is very kind of her. It is true that some parts of our county have fine vistas. Where there is mining for coal, as on parts of Adam Harford's estate, things are very different!"

"How is your mother, Mrs. Harrison?" ventured Georgiana rather diffidently.

Robert smiled at her across the table.

"My mother is as well as can be expected, thank you, and asked me to bring her good wishes, Miss Darcy. It is a very long time since she has been able to enjoy hearing her pianoforte being played with four hands, as you and I did during your visit! Have you had any success in trying the game of pell-mell here at Pemberley?"

"Not so far. Unfortunately my brother does not have any bats, balls or hoops."

"Would you like me to try to obtain some for you in London whilst I am there? I thought that you had the makings of being a fine player with a little more practice."

Georgiana blushed, and replied that he flattered her, but that she would be interested if Mr. Harrison could find a supplier in town.

Dialogue with Darcy

"I am not sure," said Fitzwilliam, "that my cousin will appreciate his sister becoming very proficient, but that will do Darcy no harm at all."

Their host had not been following the conversation, but was willing to join in the general merriment at the table.

"That is very unkind, cousin, for when did I ever prevent my sister taking an interest in any pastime if she wished to?"

After that, the rest of the evening was passed in general conversation. Darcy knew that he was provoking his wife when, as they reached their bed chamber, he said, "For a piano player, my dear, he seems to be a fine young man!"

Some months earlier, Elizabeth might have risen to this jibe, but now she realised that Robert Harrison had passed at least one test for her husband, and she was looking forward to seeing what else might transpire.

After a hearty breakfast on the following day, Mr. Harrison was taken out by Darcy and Fitzwilliam for a morning's shooting on the estate, leaving Georgiana at home to play rather disconsolately at the pianoforte.

Elizabeth, seeing her rather mournful expression, had determined to remedy the situation when the gentlemen returned to the house, but she had no need, for Robert Harrison had decided to take matters into his own hands as soon as luncheon was over.

CHAPTER EIGHT

Fitzwilliam and Darcy had gone to the library to discuss a letter recently arrived from the Earl, and Elizabeth excused herself to attend to domestic matters, leaving Georgiana with Mr. Harrison in the drawing room.

"Have you seen the Duke and Duchess recently, sir?"

"Yes, I went to see Sophie Harford two weeks ago. You may remember that she had been describing her plans for a school for the coal miners' children during your visit?"

"Yes, I do, for I was very interested in that idea."

"Well, you may be able to help me, for I have been thinking that some unused buildings on the far side of my estate could be put into a similar use. But I would need some assistance in considering matters carefully. May I explain?"

Soon they were busy discussing the requirements for making the project work, including the changes needed to the structure, ordering books and other materials, and who should be employed to teach the children.

"However, that is enough of my own concerns. I have brought something for you, Miss Darcy."

Robert Harrison went across to a side table, where he had laid some papers earlier, and brought them to show to Georgiana.

"These are some modest musical variations that I have written for each of the pieces that we played together in Yorkshire."

Georgiana was stunned that he should take so much trouble on her account.

"How very kind of you, sir. I did not realise that you are a composer as well as a musician!"

He smiled, his green eyes fixed on her face as he continued.

"That is putting my talents far too high, but I have made an attempt to elaborate on the pieces by Haydn, Mozart and Handel that we played that day, in case you might like what I have done? Can we try them together on your pianoforte? I remember you saying what a fine instrument your brother had given to you."

Georgiana could not resist such an invitation, and led the way to the music room. Taking a chair, he sat down beside her at the keyboard, and slowly played each variation in turn, before inviting her to try them herself. Hesitant at first, Georgiana soon began to play with real grace and style, and was so engrossed that she was not aware of the expression on his face as Robert watched her attentively.

Elizabeth, attracted to the doorway by the sound of the music as she passed by, was glad that Darcy was elsewhere, for there are some things that men can disrupt if they are not guided by their wives, and she slipped away before either Georgiana or her companion knew she had been there.

"You are a very fine pianist, Miss Darcy, and I hesitate to offer to join you in playing my variations with four hands!"

Georgiana was almost overcome with confusion at this remark, but then reminded herself that she had spent the morning wishing that he was with her, so it was foolish to lose this opportunity now.

"I seem to remember that you are very proficient, so please do let us play together now!"

So they did so, and there was little more conversation for some time, as he showed her some other possibilities with the tunes, and they sat side by side fully occupied in something that they both enjoyed.

Dialogue with Darcy

Elizabeth had taken the precaution of going to the library to suggest to Darcy and his cousin that the pianists were best left undisturbed until they had finished playing.

"You should remember that Georgiana had rather a dull morning whilst you gentlemen were all busy in the field."

Darcy was about to make an observation, and then caught his wife's eye and thought the better of it. So it was Fitzwilliam who said to Darcy what all of them were thinking.

"It may be none of my business, cousin, but Robert and your sister seem to be very well suited."

A few minutes later, the sound from the music room had ceased, and eventually Elizabeth went to see where Georgiana was. The music room was empty, as was the drawing room, and she eventually traced the visitor and her sister-in-law by the sound of a noise on a wooden floor, and peals of laughter coming from the picture gallery. There she saw that piles of books had been arrange to form openings through which Georgiana and her companion were directing balls made from papers pressed together, propelled by their hands.

"It's the best we could do to reproduce pell-mell," Robert Harrison explained. "I can assure you, ma'am, that we have avoided the pictures!"

Georgiana had expected a slight reprimand for her unorthodox behaviour, and Mr. Harrison was ready to apologise on her behalf, but instead Elizabeth asked if she might take a turn. It was Darcy, coming up the stairs to see what was going on, who suggested that they might all like to return to the drawing room for a rest.

There, Fitzwilliam produced the chess board, and they took turns to play short matches, with scant regard for the rules but a great deal of enjoyment, for some time.

Robert Harrison was to leave mid-morning on the following day, so the family were about to enjoy a leisurely breakfast in the dining room, and were waiting for their guest to join them, when a footman came to inform Elizabeth that he had heard a carriage arriving at the front door.

"Do you know who it is?" said Darcy.

The man replied that there was a coat of arms on the side of the vehicle, and that a lady had been brought into the hall who was asking for Mr. Harrison.

"I will go and find out," said Elizabeth, and she left her place at the table and followed the footman out of the dining-room. There in the hall was a well-dressed person who she did not recognize.

"May I help you?" said Elizabeth.

The stranger thanked her and introduced herself.

"Are you Mrs. Darcy? My name is Sophie Harford. I believe that you have met my younger sister, Harriet Maitland?"

Elizabeth acknowledged that she had, and asked if anything unfortunate had happened at Banford Hall.

"No, all is well at my father's house, but I travelled yesterday from Yorkshire, arriving very late at night, because it was necessary to get a message urgently to Robert Harrison."

"Oh, is it bad news? Mr. Harrison should be down for breakfast shortly. Let the footman take your coat and please come with me to join the family."

Sophie Harford followed Elizabeth across the hall and into the dining room on the far side. As soon as she saw the newcomer, Georgiana jumped to her feet and went across to greet her, whilst Fitzwilliam whispered quietly to Darcy, who was sitting next to him.

"Sophie, what a pleasure to see you here, but why ...?"

"Please take this seat, your Grace," said Darcy, pulling out his own chair for the guest.

Dialogue with Darcy

Sophie Harford addressed her next remark to Fitzwilliam.

"Col. Fitzwilliam, I am sorry to say that I bring bad news for your friend. His mother was taken very seriously ill very soon after he left home to travel south. When the news reached the castle, it seemed best for me to travel immediately to stay with my father last night, so that I could come to Pemberley this morning, hoping that Robert had not already left for London. I understand that he is still with you?"

"Yes," said Fitzwilliam, "and indeed here he is now," as the door opened and Robert came in.

When he saw the duchess, he stopped, and his expression changed.

"Sophie, how very good to see you, but why are you here and so early in the morning?"

She rose from her chair and went across to him.

"I am very sorry to be the bearer of bad news. Your mother has been taken ill, and the physician says that you must come as quickly as possible back to Yorkshire."

After a few more words of explanation to the assembled company about her journey, Robert Harrison turned to Darcy and Elizabeth.

"Please excuse me if I leave immediately once my bag has been packed."

"Of course," said Elizabeth, and she went to call one of the servants to help him, and another to go to find the coachman to get the Harrisons' carriage ready to carry Robert home. Then she went to ask Mrs. Reynolds to arrange for Cook to pack some food in a basket for Mr. Harrison on his return journey.

Whilst he was upstairs, Sophie Harford explained that, now she was in Derbyshire, she planned to stay for a few days with her father and sister before returning to the North.

"The reason for my being here is unfortunate indeed, but my father will be delighted if I can be with him and Harriet for a short time. Perhaps,

Georgiana, you and Fitzwilliam might like to take luncheon with us at Banford Hall later this week?"

Fitzwilliam happily accepted this invitation on their joint behalf, and soon the footman came to tell Elizabeth and Darcy that Mr Harrison's carriage was ready for him on the forecourt.

All this had happened in such a short space of time that Georgiana's mind was in a whirl. When Mr, Harrison came down the main staircase to say goodbye to the family, he ended by going across to her.

"Miss Darcy, I fear that our next game of pell-mell will have to be postponed to sometime in the future, but I promise you that I will not forget about it, or about finding you some hoops, bats and balls!"

Turning to his hosts he said, "I will write to you all as soon as there is any news. Thank you so much for your very friendly hospitality."

Then he said farewell to Sophie Harford, and hurried from the room.

"Have you had any breakfast, your Grace?" asked Georgiana.

"I must admit that I have not, for the priority seemed to be to see Robert as soon as possible. Poor man, I fear that the news will not be good when he gets home!"

"In that case, please join us for some refreshments straight away," said Elizabeth, and she asked one of the footmen to return to the kitchen to bring some new dishes for the visitor.

Soon Georgiana and their guest were deep in conversation, and the duchess was passing on all the latest news of what had been happening at the castle, including the progress of the plans for the school.

"Has Mr. Fraser finished installing the pumps for your husband yet?"

"Yes indeed. A great deal of time is being spent on adjusting them and checking on the water levels in the mines. Although my knowledge of the whole matter is limited, it does seem that the idea is a great success so far."

After she had had the opportunity to finish her meal at leisure, Sophie Harford thanked her hosts and, after saying how much she looked forward to seeing Georgiana and Fitzwilliam at Banford Hall soon, she went on her way.

Darcy and his wife had the opportunity later that morning to reflect on the visit by Sophie Harford without being overheard.

"She is not at all like Harriet Maitland, my dearest, but she seems to have a very good opinion of Georgiana and that must be good for your sister?"

"I agree, and she is clearly anxious to maintain the acquaintance, for there was no real need for the duchess to invite Fitzwilliam or Georgiana to lunch at Banford Hall before she returns to Harford Castle."

Elizabeth smiled quietly at her husband's remark, and resolved not to say that she hoped that the invitation might have been at least partly prompted by the wishes of Miss Harriet Maitland to see Fitzwilliam again.

Because of the dramatic events that morning, any thoughts of Lady Catherine and the health of her daughter Anne had been driven from their minds, but the arrival of a letter for Fitzwilliam from Rosings altered that situation.

"What does my aunt say this time?" asked Darcy, recognizing the handwriting.

His cousin, having read the unusually short note, looked up.

"In fact, there is nothing really new. Anne is no better, and perhaps a little worse, than she was. After Lady Catherine's disdain of my offer to help, she now seems more interested in my visiting Kent, but I'm not going to do that until after I had been to Banford Hall."

His firm and decisive tone of voice caught Elizabeth's attention, and he was not unaware of a questioning look, and then her quiet smile.

Dialogue with Darcy

Well, said Fitzwilliam to himself, does it really matter very much if she guesses what my real priorities are now?

When she went to bed that night, Georgiana was quite disconsolate about the unhappy turn of events that morning, and yet not quite sure why. After all, Mr. Harrison had been going to leave for London that same day in any case, and she could wait several more weeks, or even more months, to obtain a set of hoops, bats and balls for pell-mell. So what was the problem? She really could not find a reason that satisfied her.

On the morning that the two cousins were to visit Banford Hall, Darcy and Elizabeth were in her private sitting room when a letter finally arrived from Jane and Mr Bingley, announcing the date when they would be travelling north, ready to take possession of their new home in Derbyshire. Jane confirmed that her father, Mr. Bennet, would be travelling with them to stay at Pemberley with Elizabeth and Darcy.

"I should have known," observed Elizabeth, "that the quiet few weeks that we have just passed through were not likely to continue! How fine it will be to have your friend and Jane living so much closer to us."

"Yes, that is an outcome devoutly to be wished, my dearest. Do you have any plans for when your father comes to stay?"

"Well, if I can persuade Georgiana away from visiting her new-found friends like Harriet and Emily Brandon whilst he is here, I know that my Papa values her company as much as he does your own."

"I suspect that it may be my library that your father values, rather than my own company!"

Elizabeth began to object to this remark, until she realised that her dear Darcy was joking her, for she knew that in fact the two gentlemen had a great deal in common, particularly as far as their mutual love of books was concerned.

Dialogue with Darcy

"Have I ever told you, my darling girl, that my admiration for your quick wit and lively personality confounded all my prejudices after we first met, and eventually swept me into the happiest time of my life?"

"Perhaps you did, but I should never tire of you repeating that to me! I hope that you and I never lose our ability to laugh at each other, for it is my fervent wish that you do not intend to emulate the Reverend Collins!"

"That, Elizabeth, I can promise you without any risk of contradiction."

For Fitzwilliam, the journey later in the week to Banford Hall could not pass quickly enough, for he was very anxious to see Harriet again. Georgiana's motivation, although rather different, was equally strong and they were both very happy when the carriage turned off the main road and up the drive to the house.

There, they were both given a warm welcome by the Maitland family and, after some refreshments had been served, Sophie invited Georgiana to join her in walking around the garden. Lewis Maitland asked Fitzwilliam if he would be interested in seeing some information about Mr Coke's new farming practices which could be found in the library.

"Why don't we go and have a look, sir? And Harriet, you come too, for you have some knowledge of the matter."

Fitzwilliam smiled at Harriet as they followed her father across the hall, who went to the bookshelves to take down a roll of papers neatly bound together with ribbon.

"Some of these papers were given to my estate manager when he was in Norfolk, and others have been passed on to us by Harry Douglas, the father of my son-in-law Kit Hatton, who is using the same methods on his land at Norton Place."

For whatever reason, after some time Lewis Maitland left the room, leaving the two young people in the library looking through the sheaf of

147

papers together, and giving Fitzwilliam the opportunity to ask a question.

"Miss Maitland, how is your father's health?"

"He says very little about it, sir. Papa very rarely complains about anything. But on occasion, as perhaps now, he goes to lie down quietly upstairs to regain his strength."

"I hope that you will not think me impertinent if I say that, should any crisis occur and I can be of use, please do not hesitate to send for me. The welfare of your father, and your own, are important to me."

Harriet's steady gaze, so familiar and dear to him, was fixed on Fitzwilliam's face and, although a becoming blush overtook her cheeks, she did not look away, and he thought that he saw in her eyes the possibility of an attachment equal to his own.

"I am most grateful to you for saying that. I was thinking the other day what I would do if my father is taken ill, for there is little likelihood that either Sophie, or my elder sister Julia, would be anywhere nearby. Harry Douglas and his wife, if they were at home at Norton Place, would be very happy to assist, but she still has her house in Bath, and they spend quite a large part of their time there, and travelling between Julia and Kit's estate in Dorset, and Sophie and Adam at Harford Castle."

Fitzwilliam hesitated for several moments, and then decided that the time had come for action rather than words.

So he took her hands in his own, very gently, and then raised them to his lips and kissed her fingers in as neutral a manner as he could manage. She made no effort to disengage her hands from his, nor did her eyes leave his face, and there was a long silence when neither of them spoke a word.

It was with considerable difficulty that Fitzwilliam then turned his attention back to the papers that Lewis Maitland had asked him to inspect. Harriet echoed his mood, and offered some explanations of how the methods which had been so effective on Mr. Coke's estate in Norfolk had been used at Banford Hall.

When they finally returned to the drawing room, they found Sophie and Georgiana showing no signs of having missed either of them. The two ladies were deep in conversation about the latest styles of gown, the young bucks who were the talk of the town, and what the recent news was about the Brandon family at Cressborough Castle.

Lewis Maitland rejoined the party in time to take luncheon with the young people, and he asked whether there was any news from Mr. Harrison after he had left to return to Yorkshire.

"No, we have heard nothing, sir," said Georgiana, "and Sophie tells me that you have not heard anything either. I don't know whether that indicates the worst, or something else."

Her host agreed, although he said that Mrs. Harrison had been in declining in health for several years. Then they turned their conversation to happier subjects before it was time for the two cousins to return home to Pemberley.

With only a few days remaining before the Bingleys and Mr. Bennet were due to arrive from Hertfordshire, it was time for both Darcy and his wife to make preparations.

Elizabeth had been with their housekeeper Mrs. Reynolds to see the house where the Bingleys would be living, and together they had made a list of matters that might need attention urgently once the new owners arrived. With Jane expecting her first child in a few months' time, her sister wanted to avoid her over exerting herself.

Darcy had asked his estate manager to visit the Bingleys' property, and he had returned to give a full report on what he had found.

Dialogue with Darcy

Fitzwilliam, primed with his knowledge of the new farming methods being used at Banford Hall, had a long discussion with his cousin about whether they were suitable for Charles Bingley to utilise.

Georgiana, left somewhat to her own devices by all this activity, was hoping that a letter would arrive soon from Yorkshire, either from Mr. Harrison, or from Sophie Harford. However, eventually the news came via Harriet Maitland at Banford Hall.

"Whatever is the matter?" said Elizabeth, when she came upon her sister-in-law sitting at her pianoforte in the music room, but making no effort to use the keyboard, since it was obvious that Georgiana had been crying.

"Harriet has just sent word that they have heard from her sister Sophie that Robert's mother, Mrs. Harrison, died two days ago. I was just about to go and find my cousin. His friend would have liked Fitzwilliam to attend the funeral, but there will not be enough time for him to reach Yorkshire before then."

Elizabeth persuaded Georgiana to go with her to sit in the drawing room where she could put her arm around her, for there was not really space for them both to sit by side-by-side on the piano stool. When Fitzwilliam eventually came into the room with Darcy, he had almost anticipated the news, since the Harrison family had been in all their thoughts since Robert had left Pemberley.

"Harriet said to tell you, Fitzwilliam, that Mr. Harrison intends to resume his journey to London in two or three weeks' time."

"In that case, I suppose that I ought to visit Lady Catherine at Rosings straight away, and then return to Derbyshire before he gets here."

Darcy, correctly assuming that this remark was really addressed to him, replied that this seemed to be the most practical arrangement, and that Robert Harrison should be invited to stay longer for his next visit, if he wished, before continuing his journey to town.

So it was, when the Bingleys arrived with Mr Bennet at last, that Fitzwilliam was in Kent and only Georgiana was at Pemberley with Darcy and Elizabeth to welcome them. Their host asked the servants to take the luggage to the guest rooms, and Charles and Jane Bingley went up to change their travelling clothes.

Meanwhile, Elizabeth attended to her father.

"Papa, I have been so looking forward to seeing you again! How was your journey? Did you stay overnight at the George Inn in Stamford?"

"My dear, I travelled in considerable comfort with Jane and my son-in-law watching over me, but I must admit that I am very glad to have reached Pemberley."

"Let Mrs. Reynolds take you to your bedchamber now. Do you wish to rest for a while?"

"No, there is no need for that, Lizzy. I shall be down very soon to join you all."

Soon the family and their guests were busy in conversation, catching up with all the news. Jane spoke about the latest fashions from town, and Darcy and Elizabeth were able to contribute their information about the Bingleys' new house and the estate there. Georgiana took the chance to become better acquainted with Mr. Bennet, and to enjoy his quiet, dry sense of humour.

When Elizabeth finally found an opportunity to have Jane to herself, she was reassured by her sister's assurances that she had been feeling very well for the last few weeks, and that the months of sickness were behind her. Charles Bingley had been a great support, and was keenly awaiting the arrival of their first child.

"And how are Mr. Bingley's sisters?" asked Elizabeth.

"It would be accurate to say that Louisa Hurst and Caroline Bingley are not at all pleased about us moving so far north, and I have already been informed that our new home is not sufficiently grand to meet their aspirations. We shall, of course, have to invite them to visit us at some time, but I for one will not be rushing to do so!"

Elizabeth laughed out loud, for it made a change for Jane to be so precise compared to her normally easy manner and compliant attitude.

"Well, that is the future, and now at last you are both here, so surely we should all concentrate on enjoying ourselves. Darcy and I are very ready to help you settle into your new home."

"How is Georgiana? She seems to have grown more mature these past few weeks?" were Jane's next questions.

Elizabeth was cautious in her response to this, for she did not wish to reveal any information that might betray Georgiana's private thoughts, and so replied that she was well enough. So Elizabeth moved on quickly to talk about Fitzwilliam's recent journey to see his aunt and cousin in Kent.

The next topic of conversation was Mrs. Bennet's reaction to Jane's move to Derbyshire, and here clearly their father had been very happy to have the opportunity to escape for a couple of weeks from the tirade of objections to which he had recently been subjected.

It was the following afternoon before Elizabeth was able to ask her father directly about her Mama's reaction to the Bingleys' move to the north.

"I must admit, my dear Lizzy, that life at Longbourn has been very tiresome since your mother discovered that Jane and Charles Bingley were to move away from Hertfordshire, and she was even less happy when I said that they had my full support in that decision."

"Do you have a particular reason for supporting them?"

Dialogue with Darcy

"Yes. They will have no peace or privacy from your mother if they stay where they are. When your Mama was not saying what colours they should use to decorate the walls in their home, she was telling them what names they should choose for their first child, or insisting that Jane will come to harm because she is not getting enough rest! If Charles were not such a mild mannered gentleman, he would have fallen out with my wife before now. Your Darcy would have exploded with rage long since, and he would have been quite right!"

"So," said his daughter mischievously, "I assume that you will not be in a great hurry to go home to Longbourn?"

Mr. Bennet smiled wearily.

"If I was not of the opinion that Mary and Kitty will be at their wit's end if I do not return at the end of the month, I would stay as long as you would have me here. But they are young, and should be getting out to visit their friends, meeting new people and enjoying themselves, not attending to their mother's complaints."

Elizabeth was inclined to doubt whether her sister Mary, always engrossed in her books or playing another serious piece on her piano, was likely to be seeking a marriage partner, but her younger sister was a different matter.

"I suppose that Kitty still wants to go to stay with Lydia and Wickham?"

"Yes, and her mother supports her foolish notion, but I have absolutely no intention of agreeing to that."

And they smiled at each other with mutual understanding.

"Did you have any opportunity for a private conversation with Charlotte Collins whilst she was staying with her parents? You said very little in your letter, beyond how long she had been in Hertfordshire before returning to London."

Dialogue with Darcy

"I am glad that you mention that, my dear, for I did have an unexpected chance to speak with her. Your Mama had gone to Meryton with your sister Kitty, and Mary was busy with her music as usual, when Charlotte called at Longbourn on her last afternoon to say goodbye to our family. So we had the chance to talk together for about an hour before we were interrupted."

"I am glad about that, Papa."

"She was very tactful, but I would guess that life with the Reverend Collins is just as tiresome as you have always suspected would be the case. Certainly, Charlotte had been very happy to be summoned by Lady Catherine to accompany her to town, as a rare chance to get away from Rosings for a week or two. Apparently her husband had offered to travel with them, but Lady Catherine would have none of it, saying that he was needed to stay behind to tend to his parishioners. So Charlotte was very grateful for that intervention!"

Elizabeth laughed, for she could recall how Lady Catherine liked to be of use, or at least always to dictate what other people should do.

"What your friend did tell me during our conversation was rather unexpected. Whilst she was staying at Brook Street, and before the Earl and his wife arrived from Essex, Anne de Bourgh was in bed asleep one day after a visit from the doctor. Charlotte was sitting alone with Lady Catherine to keep her company when she started talking about what she might do if her daughter did not live much longer."

"Oh, how very sad!"

"Yes, you could well say so. Apparently the Rosings estate is entailed to a distant cousin, although Lady Catherine has the right to choose whether to remain there during her lifetime."

"Yes, Darcy has told me that."

"But I recall from what you said after your visit to Kent last year that the mansion there is enormous – perhaps not as extensive as the

Dialogue with Darcy

Reverend Collins might like to suggest, but still very large for a lady to want to live on her own, without any family."

"It is certainly a property with very many rooms."

"Lady Catherine told Charlotte that she is not on speaking terms with the heir to the estate, which will not surprise you in the least, and in some ways she would be very unwilling to grant him any favours. However, she is obviously giving some thought to moving elsewhere if the worst happens to her daughter Anne, and Derbyshire would be one possibility."

Elizabeth exclaimed at the very thought of this suggestion, and her father patted her hand.

"No, I did not think that you would favour that option, Lizzy, or Darcy either, I would wager?"

"No, indeed not. I cannot think of anything that he would dislike more!"

"Lady Catherine said that she could supervise Georgiana more easily if she lived much closer to Pemberley! She seemed to be of the opinion that she would be doing Darcy a favour in that regard."

Elizabeth knew very well what her sister-in-law would make of that idea.

"Georgiana is an adult now, and has no need of anyone but her brother and myself to advise her. You know how she and I have become so close since I married my dear Mr. Darcy!"

"Well, you may all escape the fate that Lady Catherine has in store for you, for she also spoke of moving to Hertfordshire to be near the Earl and his family, which of course was where she lived for many years as a child and until she was married."

"Did Charlotte say anything else to you?"

Her father hesitated.

"Only that she envied you, and hopes that you still have as independent an attitude to life as ever you had!"

Dialogue with Darcy

This remark brought Elizabeth up short, and made her feel very sad, for she had been so happy since her marriage and moving to Derbyshire that she had not really considered independence to be so important.

"Cheer up, Lizzy, for we both know that Charlotte made a conscious choice to marry for security, rather than stay single and be dependent on her parents and younger brother in the future. By the way, Kitty asked me to tell you that Charlotte's sister, Maria Lucas, has a new and very promising admirer."

"Oh, who is that?" said Elizabeth, keen to change to a happier subject.

"Some young blade who is the brother of the estate manager at Netherfield, the house that Bingley had been renting near us. Kitty seems to think that it might come to something, and Lady Lucas is busy encouraging the match."

Elizabeth could well imagine that, and her own mother making herself busy spreading the news all around Meryton.

Mr. Bennet seemed to enjoy his stay at Pemberley. Bingley and Jane took him to inspect their new home, where preparations for them moving in to take possession were going well. Georgiana was happy to be an honorary daughter, and Mr. Bennet was willing to sit in the music room reading whilst she played the pianoforte because, as he told Elizabeth mischievously, Georgiana was at least as proficient a pianist as his daughter Mary!

There was at one point a suggestion from Fitzwilliam that he might take Elizabeth and Mr. Bennet to visit Lewis Maitland at Banford Hall, since they shared a love of books, but Harriet sent a note by return to say that her father had taken a chill, and was not well enough to receive visitors, however congenial they might be.

However, by various means the visitor was kept well entertained until the day came for

Elizabeth to take him back to Hertfordshire in the family's carriage.

"I shall be sorry not to see you both settled in your new home before I go," Mr. Bennet remarked to Bingley and Jane, as the luggage was being loaded onto the carriage.

"We have to keep something for you to look forward to during your next visit, sir," Darcy observed.

Then, after handing his father-in-law into the carriage, Darcy drew Elizabeth aside to say a quiet but loving farewell to his wife.

"Write to me, my darling Elizabeth, as soon as you arrive safely at Longbourn, and hurry back, for I shall miss you so much. I doubt if I will ever become accustomed to you not being here with me at Pemberley!"

Dialogue with Darcy

CHAPTER NINE

The journey to Longbourn passed without incident, and Elizabeth and her father spent the time pleasantly in conversation about their family and friends. Mr. Bennet raised the subject of his daughter, Kitty, and asked Elizabeth for her advice.

"Lizzy, I can recall very well that you were right and I was wrong about your sister Lydia's behaviour last year. What should I do about Kitty, especially in the event that her best friend Maria Lucas was to marry and move away?"

"We must wish Maria well in that case, but I wonder, since Kitty does not have any other close friends in the area, whether it might be an idea for her to come and stay with us for a few weeks? Darcy's sister Georgiana has a good circle of acquaintances in Derbyshire, and I'm sure if I asked her that she would take my sister to visit some of them."

Mr. Bennet said that such an offer would be more than generous, and he anticipated that Kitty would accept it immediately.

"Mind you, your mother might take a very different view, since we would be removing your sister from her control and supervision! I don't imagine that Mary would worry one way or the other whether Kitty was at Longbourn. Why don't you have a quiet conversation with Kitty when we get back to Hertfordshire, and see what she thinks? Or would you rather speak to Mr. Darcy first?"

"That is not necessary, Papa, for my dear husband did suggest some months ago that Kitty might benefit from getting away from Longbourn.

159

Dialogue with Darcy

Oh, perhaps I put that rather badly. I meant that what my sister needs is a change of scene and to have a chance to see more of the world."

So it was agreed that the matter should be raised during Elizabeth's relatively brief stay with her parents. When they arrived at Longbourn, to an extravagantly emotional welcome from Mrs. Bennet, it was to find Elizabeth's aunt, Mrs. Gardiner, already there. She had been staying for a few days with her sister-in-law, and was due to return to London on the following day. Their aunt had always been a good friend to her elder two nieces, and Elizabeth was especially pleased to see her because of the significant role that she had played in Darcy and his wife being united.

"Dear Aunt, how delightful that you are here. How are you, and what is the news of Mr. Gardiner and the children? Is all well in Gracechurch Street?"

"Dear Lizzy, yes, of course, we are all very well."

"I am not very well at all, Lizzy," interjected her mother who was standing beside her. "How can I be happy when Jane and Mr. Bingley have suddenly given up their house at Netherfield, and moved so far away to Derbyshire?"

"But Mama, you still have Mary and Kitty here to console you, and now Papa is back at Longbourn?"

Mrs. Bennet sniffed, and indicated that Mr. Bennet's presence was very unlikely to improve the situation. As for her younger daughters, their company did not compare to that of her eldest daughter and new son-in-law.

When Mrs. Gardiner eventually found an opportunity for some quiet conversation with her niece, Elizabeth was regaled with an entertaining account of Mrs. Bennet's woes and complaints. These extended also to the refusal of her husband to either entertain a visit from George Wickham and his wife Lydia, or to allow Mrs.

160

Bennet or either of her younger daughters to travel north to see the couple at the regiment's headquarters.

"Papa is quite right," said Elizabeth, "for Lydia will always be a very unfortunate influence on the others. I very much doubt whether Mary would be remotely interested in visiting the regiment and meeting the officers there, but Kitty might be more susceptible to the attractions of a military uniform."

Her aunt agreed, and Elizabeth then raised the possibility of Kitty travelling north with her on the return journey to Derbyshire.

"What would Mr. Darcy's view of that idea be, Lizzy? Have you ever discussed the subject?"

"As it happens, yes, we have. Darcy had been talking with Georgiana about my sisters, and she had suggested that Kitty might like to come to stay with us for a few weeks. So all I need to do is to write a line to my dear husband, to say that I will be returning with my sister."

Following this conversation, Elizabeth took the chance to talk to Kitty about the idea, which was received with great enthusiasm, and her elder sister had to caution her a little by saying that both her parents would need to agree. When advised of the suggestion, Mrs. Bennet was torn between the great advantages that she could anticipate for Kitty in staying in such a grand household, and the fact that she herself would be left with only Mary, her studious daughter, for company, a young lady with whom she had very little in common.

But Mrs. Bennet's opinion was swayed by Mrs. Gardiner supporting the proposal, and by her sister-in-law emphasising the grand surroundings in which Kitty would find herself. Mrs. Gardiner recalled her visit to Derbyshire the previous year, and the gracious reception that she and her husband had received from Mr. Darcy and his sister Georgiana.

Dialogue with Darcy

As Mrs. Gardiner left for London next morning, she promised Elizabeth that she would make every effort to persuade her husband that her family should travel north for a short visit to Pemberley very soon.

A letter arrived for Mr. Bennet from his daughter Jane in Derbyshire, to say that the Bingleys were in the process of moving from Pemberley into their new home.

"I suggest," he said to Elizabeth, "that since your Mama was in Meryton with Kitty and Mary when the post came, we will not mention this news to her for the present. Otherwise, she will be troubling your sister Jane and your brother-in-law with demands to visit them before they have had time to settle!"

"Sadly, you are quite right, Papa, and I am sure that they would prefer to postpone any visit from Mama to later in the year, perhaps after their child has been born."

Elizabeth spent the rest of her short stay at Longbourn sharing her time between her mother and her father. She had anticipated that Mary might be rather resentful of the fact that Kitty was going to be staying with the Darcys at Pemberley, but that young lady seemed to prefer the opportunity to be spared the frivolities of her sister Kitty's company, and have a rare chance to be the only daughter left at home.

Mr. Bennet parted with Elizabeth with his habitual assurance that life at Longbourn without her would resume its usual tedium.

"For you know, Lizzy, how fixated your Mama can be on matters of no interest to me whatsoever! But never mind, for I shall be consoled by having seen how happy you are in your new environment, and I hope to be invited to Pemberley again in the not too distant future!"

Mrs. Bennet kept herself busy for the last day of Elizabeth's stay in making sure that Kitty would be taking with her an appropriate choice of dresses for any occasion to which she might be invited. Elizabeth tried, without success, to remind her mother that for most of the time her daughter would be staying in the house at Pemberley, and would not be attending a constant round of balls and other entertainments.

Whatever Kitty might think about her choice of gowns, she was consulted very little, and it was with some relief that the two sisters were eventually settled in the Darcys' carriage ready for the return journey, and set off for Derbyshire.

"I do wish," said Kitty, "that Papa would agree for me to go and visit Lydia and Wickham after I have stayed with you at Pemberley."

"I cannot agree with you, Kitty. Papa is not going to take a different view, since that is not the kind of life that you should be wishing to lead. You will meet many more interesting people when you stay with us in Derbyshire."

And with that, her younger sister had to be content, since she knew that Lizzy was not likely to change her mind.

Darcy and Elizabeth had a joyful reunion on her return to Pemberley, and Kitty was given a warm welcome by Georgiana and her brother-in-law.

"How did the move go for the Bingleys last week?" Elizabeth asked Darcy.

"Very well, I understand. Jane asked Georgiana to visit the house yesterday for tea, and I sent our housekeeper with her in case she could be of use to your sister. Mrs. Reynolds told me on her return that that the furniture is all placed where it should be, and the new staff that have been hired are doing well enough for now! Jane has suggested that Kitty might like to stay there for a few days, before she has to return to Longbourn."

"As soon as we heard from Elizabeth that you would be coming," said Georgiana, "I have been planning various entertainments and outings for you, Kitty. Tomorrow, we shall be going to

Cressborough Castle. There we will meet my friends Emily Brandon and Harriet Maitland, and perhaps Emily's aunt and uncle, the Earl and Countess, if they are at home."

"Oh!" exclaimed Kitty, completely overwhelmed by the idea of visiting a castle and its titled owners. She was delighted at this prospect, and the various other opportunities that were being suggested to occupy her during her stay.

After her rather tiring journey, Elizabeth was very happy to have the chance for a peaceful day at home with Darcy whilst Georgiana and Kitty spent the day at Cressborough.

"Did you miss me a little?" she asked him rather shyly.

"No, not a little – a very great deal, my darling! The house seemed so empty without you being here with me, although I did my best to keep busy as you had suggested. However delightful Georgiana may be, she is no substitute at all for you!"

Elizabeth held his hand tightly, and he put his arm around her and clasped her close.

"Has there been any news from Fitzwilliam?"

"Yes, he is now on his way back to town from Kent, and will arrive here after a couple of days staying at Brook Street at his brother's house. He wrote in his letter that Anne de Bourgh is very unwell, but he sat and read to her every day at Rosings, which she seemed to enjoy."

"And Lady Catherine ...?"

"I gather that her manner of speaking was largely unchanged, but Fitzwilliam sensed an added vulnerability behind her gruff manner."

Poor woman, thought Elizabeth, how very powerless she must feel, and she would absolutely hate that. But Darcy had other news to impart.

"Fitzwilliam asked me to open any letter that should arrive for him here from Yorkshire, and one came at the beginning of this week. Robert

Dialogue with Darcy

Harrison wrote that he hopes to resume his journey from Yorkshire to London within the next few weeks, and would write again to say when he hopes to get here. Georgiana seemed to welcome that news, although I very much doubt that he will arrive with a set of pell-mell bats, hoops, and balls for her!"

No, probably not, thought Elizabeth, but I suspect that it is Robert Harrison she looks forward to seeing, rather than what he might bring with him.

Their conversation then turned to the household at Longbourn, and Mrs. Bennet's state of mind. Elizabeth explained that Mrs. Gardiner had been there when she arrived, and had asked to be remembered to Darcy.

"Kitty seems to be very pleased to be here with us, my dear."

"Yes, indeed, and Papa was very grateful to know that you would be happy about that. Georgiana seems to have been very busy since she received my letter, making arrangements to keep my sister occupied!"

"She has enjoyed making various arrangements, and don't forget that she will be involved in those herself as well! As you have pointed out from time to time, when there are no visitors staying with us, life can be rather dull for Georgiana."

Elizabeth smiled, and agreed, for she could remember how boring life at Longbourn had been for the same reason, enlivened only by visiting Charlotte Lucas, going to the occasional ball at Meryton, or anticipating the arrival of the regiment.

When they returned together from Cressborough Castle, Kitty and Georgiana were full of stories about everything that had happened during the day. Emily Brandon had been a charming hostess, and had showed them round many of the state rooms in the castle. Kitty had been almost overcome with shyness when the Countess had joined them for luncheon, although her ladyship had been very gracious. Georgiana had been particularly delighted when Harriet Maitland had arrived to be with them for the rest of the afternoon. The final high point of the day had been when the Earl himself had joined them in the drawing room towards the end of their visit, and had invited Georgiana and Kitty to view the picture gallery with him.

"I really must write to Mama straight away," said Kitty to Elizabeth, "to tell her absolutely everything. Will you or Mr. Darcy mind if I retire to bed early to write a letter about the day?"

Her sister doubted whether Kitty would be able to sleep well that night after all the excitement, but agreed that the letter should be finished before she forgot everything that had occurred at Cressborough Castle.

"Before you go, Kitty, I should tell you that we have one other visitor expected here soon," said Darcy. "Mr. Fraser, an engineer who has been advising me on draining some of the land on our estate here, has written to say that he will be here in a couple of days' time to advise me on installing a second pump."

Darcy went on to explain that Mr. Fraser was a very pleasant young man, an enthusiast full of the technicalities of his business, and that Georgiana had found him to be good company.

"He will," added Elizabeth, "at the least be another new person for you to meet."

His wife was pleased to see Darcy taking particular pains during the next couple of days to become more acquainted with Kitty. Contrary to his previous opinion, underneath her rather childish manner he found that there was quite a sensible young lady who was prepared to take an interest in anything that he chose to explain to her. Kitty had quite a good sense of humour, and was very willing to take advice from Georgiana on which of her gowns suited her best, and were appropriate for particular social situations.

"I am very grateful to you, sir, and" said Elizabeth, "for taking the trouble to get to know my sister better. She takes very careful note of what you say to her, and is mightily impressed by your home and your estate!"

"Perhaps what you mean," he said wickedly, "is that Kitty is not as inclined to provoke me as a certain another young lady that I can recall lived at Longbourn, who never hesitated to challenge me if I said anything that she did not agree with!"

Elizabeth had to concede that there were some significant differences between her and Kitty that he might easily be able to identify.

"Are you suggesting that it might be better for me to become rather less querulous, and more forgiving of everything you say?"

"On reflection, I believe that I might find that exceedingly worrying, for the young lady that I fell in love with last year has never been dull company, or failed to challenge me, and she is often quite correct in what she says!"

Elizabeth was rather disconcerted by this remark.

"Does that mean that you find Kitty rather dull company? She is still quite young, and has had little opportunity to go out into the world."

Darcy assured his wife that he did not find her younger sister uninteresting, although perhaps he had thought that might be possible before she had arrived to stay with them. Rather, her character was proving to be more attractive than he had imagined on first acquaintance.

When Mr. Fraser arrived, as full of enthusiasm as ever, Georgiana's first question to him over luncheon was how his work was progressing in the mines at Harford Castle. He told them that the Duke was very happy with what had been done so far, and was considering installing several more machines, if the project continued to be as successful as was the case at the moment.

"I believe that my brother is wanting you to install more pumps here also, Mr. Fraser? Will those be different from the one that we already have here on the estate?"

"Yes, Miss Darcy, we are continually refining the design of our machines, so that they are stronger and have a greater pumping capacity."

"We must not talk about technical matters all the time," said Elizabeth, as her younger sister's expression had become more bemused during this conversation.

"Perhaps Miss Bennet might like me to explain in detail how the pumps work?" replied Mr. Fraser

"I doubt if that will be necessary," said Darcy quickly, having noticed his wife's expression on hearing the engineer's continuing enthusiasm for a new audience. "Why don't we invite Kitty to go with us in the morning when we investigate what needs to be done, and Georgiana can also accompany us if she would like to."

The outcome of this conversation the following day was a very peaceful morning for Elizabeth, for all the others had gone with Mr. Fraser to look at alternative sites for a new pump. The seamstress had been summoned to sew the drapes for the windows on each side of her desk overlooking the lake, and with the help of Mrs. Reynolds and one of the maids, good progress was made. By the time that her husband and his companions returned in the middle of the afternoon, having been fortified by a light luncheon from a basket taken to them by one of the footmen, the work on the drapes was almost completed.

Elizabeth had expected that Kitty would come back to the house with her mind full of machinery and pumps, and how they should be used, and devoutly wishing never to hear anything about them again. However, when they returned, it was clear that her younger sister had found the engineer to be congenial company. Elizabeth's doubts before his arrival as to whether Kitty and Mr. Fraser would have very much in common at all were proved to be wrong.

When Georgiana found Elizabeth in the drawing room later that evening, before the others came down to join them at dinner, she commented on this.

"I'm sure that I always have found Mr. Fraser to be very pleasant, Elizabeth, but I have never seen him look at me as he was looking at Kitty today. She is a very pleasant girl, to be sure, but I had not expected that we might find ourselves with a happy couple on our hands so soon!"

"Are you certain about that, Georgiana? They have only been in each other's company for a few hours. In any case, there are two sides to every romance, you know."

"Well, I am telling you only one side of the story, but it was so very obvious that Mr. Fraser was immediately smitten with Kitty. You know your sister much better than I do, so I will leave it to you to find out whether the attraction is mutual."

When Darcy and Elizabeth discussed the subject later that evening in the privacy of their bedchamber, he clearly had noticed that something was going on, and asked his wife to comment.

"I have heard of instant attraction, my dearest, but Kitty is nowhere nearly as sensible as you are. Has she said anything to you?"

"No, and she is not experienced in the ways of the world, so I daresay that she does not realise as clearly as Georgiana seems to that Mr. Fraser might be smitten. Let's see what happens, for he is staying until the day after tomorrow, and she will have some opportunities before he leaves to meet him again."

Dialogue with Darcy

Elizabeth was rather surprised that Darcy seemed to be so complacent about Mr. Fraser as a possible partner for her own sister; for she was certain that he would take a different view if Georgiana had been the young lady in question. Kitty, on the other hand, had neither a substantial dowry nor illustrious family connections, so perhaps Darcy was merely being pragmatic. As for herself, she admired Mr. Fraser's apparent ability to charm young ladies of quality with his, to her, rather endless recitation of matters technical!

"May I ask what you are thinking about, my dearest? You are very silent."

"Only that Mr. Fraser will be a lucky man if he can charm my sister," she said, editing the truth.

The more conversation that he had with Kitty, the more Darcy came to the view that she was a sensible young woman, albeit with a limited interest in various pursuits compared to her two elder sisters, and might make somebody a very suitable wife. Away from her mother's influence, Miss Bennet had rapidly shed her frivolous approach to life, and had done her best to fit into the very different social milieu at Pemberley.

Elizabeth took the opportunity whilst her sister was staying with them of explaining the details of how the inside staff in a large house should be managed, acknowledging that she herself had had to learn this in a very short time after her marriage to Mr. Darcy.

The housekeeper, Mrs. Reynolds, was initially rather wary of Kitty, but soon found that her personality had little in common with the rather persistent character of her mother, Mrs. Bennet.

"I wonder, if she has time," said Kitty, "whether Mrs Reynolds would explain to me how the maids produce such beautifully ironed cloths for the dining table. I cannot recall us achieving such a high standard ever at Longbourn."

Dialogue with Darcy

"I am sure that our housekeeper would be only too delighted to be complimented on the standards that she oversees here, Kitty, so do not hesitate to ask her."

Darcy, when told about this enquiry by his wife, was inclined to be amused, but Elizabeth pointed out to him that whatever domestic situation her sister might find herself in after marriage would be unlikely to include the number of maidservants that they had at Pemberley. So it was prudent for Kitty to discover how she might achieve the same results herself, or with only an untrained young girl to help her.

Meanwhile, Mr. Fraser's visit was coming to an end, and his interest in Kitty did not seem to be waning.

"I shall be travelling from Manchester towards London soon, Miss Bennet. I wonder if I might call in to your home in Hertfordshire to renew our acquaintance, if that would be acceptable to your parents?"

Kitty clearly did not realise what a remark of this kind might infer. However, she looked quickly towards Elizabeth, who was sitting opposite them in the drawing room when this question was posed, and was reassured by a barely perceptible nod of her head.

"That would be very pleasant, sir. I would be happy to give you directions to find Longbourn from our local town of Meryton. Do you know when your journey might be, so that I can tell my father?"

"I hope that it will be very soon, by the middle of next month," replied the engineer.

Knowing that Fitzwilliam was due to arrive back at Pemberley soon after the engineer would be completing his visit, Elizabeth had suggested to Georgiana that a note might be sent to Banford Hall to invite Harriet Maitland to come to Pemberley in a few days' time, whilst Kitty was still staying with them. The two young ladies were enthusiastic about this proposal, and only regretted that Emily Brandon had gone to town with her aunt and uncle, and so would not be able to join them.

"Miss Maitland is a very charming young lady," said Mr. Fraser, recalling meeting her at Harford Castle, "although she did not seem to be very interested in pumps or machinery."

This remark made Elizabeth smile, and even more so when Kitty said, "I wonder why that would be, for I find them very interesting!"

"We cannot all be the same," said Darcy, echoing his wife's smile, "but I'm sure that Mr. Fraser appreciates your taking such an interest, Kitty!"

The engineer was quick to agree with this sentiment, and entered into a discussion with Darcy and her sister that soon persuaded Elizabeth not to pursue the subject further.

Having had a final discussion with Mr Darcy on the following morning, Mr. Fraser came to find Elizabeth, Georgiana and Kitty to say goodbye. He repeated his promise to visit the Bennet family at Longbourn, and thanked his hostess for her hospitality during his stay.

"Life will be quite dull for us once you have gone," said Elizabeth, "and I'm sure that we are all much more knowledgeable about your pumps and your expertise after your visit!"

The engineer was flattered by these comments, and thanked her before settling himself in Darcy's carriage, which was to take him to the coaching inn at Buxton to continue the remainder of his journey back to Manchester.

Speaking to her husband later in the privacy of their room, Elizabeth remarked that, however pleasant their visitor had been, conversation with him was often exhausting because he so quickly lapsed into speaking of technicalities.

"That may be so, my dearest, but he is very knowledgeable about his subject, and he has clearly gained an enthusiastic adherent in your sister Kitty. I think you should write to your father in Hertfordshire to warn him, no, I mean advise him, that there is a possibility that he might be gaining a new son-in-law!"

"Do you really mean that, sir?"

"Yes, I do, but the question I must ask you is what Kitty's position may be of the matter?"

"She has said nothing to me directly, but I suspect that when she gets home she may find she has feelings for that young man that she has not yet acknowledged to herself. All I shall say to her before she leaves here at the end of the week is that Kitty should write to me once she gets home."

Darcy, as often was the case since his marriage, was taken by his wife's sensible approach to what for him might have been a difficult problem, and kissed her hand without telling her why.

Hardly had Mr Fraser departed than it was time for Fitzwilliam to arrive from town, with news of Lady Catherine and Anne de Bourgh in Kent. Georgiana gave him little time to settle into his room and change from his travelling clothes before she was full of the impending visit from Harriet Maitland. As Elizabeth had expected, this was welcome news for Fitzwilliam.

"We are really asking Harriet so that she can meet Kitty here, but it will be an opportunity to hear the news from Yorkshire before your friend Mr Harrison arrives, and to ask about what is happening at Harford Castle."

"In her reply, did Miss Maitland make any remark about the health of her father?"

"No, Fitzwilliam, she did not mention that, although I did hear from Emily Brandon a week or so ago that he had recovered from his chill and was able to walk in the garden."

Elizabeth had been watching Fitzwilliam's expression carefully during this exchange, and he was not unaware of that.

Dialogue with Darcy

"Tell us what has been happening at Rosings," said Darcy.

"In some ways, there is little change in the situation. However, although I am no expert in matters of health, it is very easy to see that our cousin Anne is now almost entirely confined to bed, and often has difficulty in getting her breath. Lady Catherine reacts to that by becoming even more irascible than usual but, as you know, I have always found it easier not to argue with her directly."

"You are right, Fitzwilliam. I daresay that Georgiana would take the same approach if she had been there. I fear that I do not have the same level of self-control. What would you have said, Elizabeth?"

"I suppose it is not so simple for me, having only a limited acquaintance with your aunt, to know how I might react, especially now that I know that she is in the middle of such a sad situation. You will recall that I found it only too easy to argue with her when I was in Kent, not to mention our famous interview at Longbourn last year!"

In general, Fitzwilliam seemed to be very cheerful, especially once he had heard that Harriet Maitland would be visiting them very soon. Yes, said Elizabeth to herself, we have finally found someone who he really cares for, and now that all that has to be solved is where and by what means they would live.

Fitzwilliam was always pleasant in conversation with people who he had only met briefly, and quickly made the effort to treat Miss Bennet as a member of the family. Kitty, once she overcame her initial shyness of him, became quite talkative. She even confided in Fitzwilliam, when there was no-one else to overhear, that she had thought Mr. Fraser to be a very handsome gentleman, and that the engineer had been exceptionally nice to her.

Dialogue with Darcy

"I am not remotely surprised about that," replied Fitzwilliam, "for Mr. Fraser would have to have had a heart of stone not to appreciate a young lady of quality such as you!"

This remark caused Kitty to blush to the roots of her hair, but secretly she realised that she was delighted.

However, Fitzwilliam's main priority was to speak to Harriet Maitland as soon as possible when she came to Pemberley a couple of days' later. He was resigned to Georgiana wanting to spend most of the day with Harriet and Kitty. However, Elizabeth had spoken to her sister-in-law briefly the previous evening, so that Georgiana included Fitzwilliam in their conversations, and took Kitty off for an hour after luncheon to look at the latest dress designs in the ladies' magazines.

Left alone with her, Fitzwilliam did not waste his opportunity and, after politely enquiring about her father's health, asked Harriet about her own state of mind. She was more frank than he had expected in her reply.

"I have been feeling rather low, sir, perhaps because Papa has been quite unwell from time to time. I cannot tell you what a lift it is to my spirits for me to be at Pemberley today."

"I am going to be rather selfish in asking whether it makes any difference to you that I am here? I should tell you that I have been looking forward to this day since I last saw you. I really cannot envisage being truly happy in the future without – without seeing you very often."

Harriet regarded him with her straight gaze for what seemed like an eternity.

"Is that, it sounds tantamount to ..."

This time it was Fitzwilliam's turn to hesitate, albeit briefly, but he had not been an officer in the army for nothing, when he had often needed to take quick decisions.

"I apologise for seeming to fudge the issue. I should be brave and tell you now that it is my dearest wish that you should become my wife. I have never felt for anyone the love and affection that I have for you. I am prepared to be patient if you do not yet know your own mind. Please tell me what is in your heart!"

Harriet paused and, instead of speaking immediately, she looked at Fitzwilliam for a few moments. Then she slowly held out one of her hands to him without shyness, but calmly and confidently, and he took it between his own. After what seemed to him to be a very long pause, Harriet replied.

"I have been thinking about you, sir, so very often during the past few weeks. I have come to the conclusion that I cannot foresee any real happiness for me in the future unless you should care for me. If you do, that is just – just wonderful!"

There are times in a gentleman's life when the proprieties must be set aside, and Fitzwilliam took Harriet into his arms and kissed her gently but persistently until she had very little breath left. Then he held her head against his shoulder, her hair soft against his neck, and whispered endearments into her ear.

After a while, they began to discuss their plans for the future, and talk about her father's health. Fitzwilliam explained to Harriet that he might soon have to travel south to Kent if the worst were to happen to his cousin Anne at Rosings.

"Your aunt Lady Catherine de Bourgh sounds to be a rather formidable person?"

"That should not matter to you one way or the other, my dearest Harriet, for she has no hold over me beyond my feeling some sympathy for a relative in trouble. Darcy will tell you that she would like to control her nephews and her niece Georgiana, but in truth her only power is to try to tell us what to do with our lives, but without success!"

Dialogue with Darcy

Harriet was not entirely convinced, but was willing to accept Fitzwilliam's advice to ask Elizabeth Darcy for her opinion.

"I should like to visit Banford Hall as soon as possible, Harriet, to ask your father formally for his blessing. Then I can go down on one knee and ask you to marry me properly, as I should have done already!"

Harriet smiled at this remark, but agreed that Lewis Maitland should be told within the next few days, and that in the meantime the happy news should be a secret between the two of them.

"I must not pretend, Harriet, that I know what our immediate future holds, for I am not wealthy like some of your friends, or the heir to a grand estate."

"I care nothing for that, sir. Money will never be equivalent to happiness in my eyes. Would you be willing to live with me after we are married at Banford Hall as long as my father survives? As you may know, because my brother is no longer with us, the estate is entailed to my distant cousin Adam after Papa's death."

"Yes, of course, if that is what you desire, Harriet, but it is not for me to make your father's choices for him."

By the time that Georgiana and Kitty rejoined them with Elizabeth and Darcy for refreshments at the end of the afternoon, Harriet and Fitzwilliam had agreed that a good reason for him to travel to Banford Hall would be to discuss the agricultural improvements on the estate there, so that Fitzwilliam could pass the information on to his brother the Earl in Essex.

The rest of the day passed without incident, and the lovers gave no clue to the rest of the family about what had occurred. Indeed, they gave Elizabeth the impression that perhaps there was less interest between Fitzwilliam and Harriet than she had previously thought, which made her rather sad, for she had grown very fond of Darcy's cousin.

CHAPTER TEN

Georgiana took Kitty with her to Buxton on the following morning to make some purchases in the shops there. From there, the carriage went on to the Bingleys' new home, where Kitty was to stay for two nights. There Georgiana took tea with the family before she was due to continue her journey back to Pemberley.

"Elizabeth asked me to say that she hears that your parents are both in good health, but that Mrs. Bennet does not yet know that you have moved into the house here. Perhaps you could take us on a quick tour before I have to leave?"

Both she and Kitty was very impressed with Jane and Bingley's new home, and Kitty asked Georgiana to pass this message back to Elizabeth.

Whilst they had their house to themselves, Darcy and his wife had been discussing the best means by which her younger sister could return to Hertfordshire in due course. One option was for Elizabeth's personal maid to travel with her by the post. Another would be for Fitzwilliam to escort Kitty in Darcy's carriage, and then carry on to visit his brother's family in Essex.

Fitzwilliam was not included in this discussion because he had acted quickly on his agreement with Harriet. As it was a very pleasant day, rather than use a carriage he had borrowed one of Darcy's best hunters to ride on the relatively short journey to see her father.

When he arrived at Banford Hall, he took his mount round to the stables where a manservant took charge of the animal for him. Fitzwilliam

179

then walked back to the front door, and was swiftly admitted to the house. He found Lewis Maitland sitting on a comfortable chair in the drawing room. He looked cheerful, although with a rather pale complexion. Harriet was standing by the window, looking happy and a little nervous at the same time.

"My daughter tells me that you are here to ask for advice about the management of the estate here, based on the principles established by Mr. Coke in Norfolk?"

"That is true, but there is something else that I would like to raise first, and I believe that the convention is that I should do so without Miss Maitland being present."

Harriet smiled at Fitzwilliam, and then quietly excused herself from the room before her father could protest. Lewis Maitland watched her go, and then turned to their guest with perhaps a growing realisation of what was to come.

"May I ask first, sir, how you are? You mentioned when we last met that your physician had been advising you about your health."

The older man sighed, and shifted in his seat.

"You are very civil, Col. Fitzwilliam, but there is really nothing to add to what I told you at Pemberley. When I get a chill, it seems to take me too much time to shake it off. Fortunately Harriet rarely catches any illness from me. Please sit down and tell me what you wish to say."

However, Fitzwilliam felt more comfortable standing, although he was glad to have the back of the settee on which to rest one of his hands.

"You may recall our conversation some time ago at Pemberley, sir, about your daughter and my intentions towards her. You were quite right, although at that time I had no inkling of Harriet's views on the matter. That situation has changed, and I am here today to ask formally for your consent to my marriage with your daughter.

180

I am very happy to say that she has told me that she reciprocates my love and affection for her."

Lewis Maitland looked down at his hands for several moments, and there was a pause. Then he raised his head and smiled at Fitzwilliam.

"I can truly say that what you tell me is excellent news. A father is perhaps not supposed to notice such things but, when Harriet returned from visiting Darcy's house yesterday, I suspected that something had occurred, although she tried almost successfully to conceal it."

Hearing these friendly words, Fitzwilliam relaxed and, looking down at his own hands, he realised that he had clasped them so tightly that his knuckles were white.

"In that case," he said, smiling at Lewis Maitland, "I will accept your invitation and sit down now."

After he had done so, and before he could continue, his host intervened.

"I suppose that the next question I should ask you, Col. Fitzwilliam, or perhaps I should ask you both, is where you intend to live?"

"Yes sir, that is a very valid enquiry, and something that Harriet and I have discussed. Your daughter would like to be here, living with you at Banford Hall."

"And you, sir, what do you prefer to do?"

"I would like to hear your comments on that suggestion before I answer you."

Lewis Maitland was tempted to say that they might have reached an impasse but then, realising that his guest was still rather nervous, he did not pursue that thought.

"Then my answer is that I would be very happy if you both choose to live here with me as a married couple, and I should be even happier if you both decide to marry quite soon. As I have already told you, my own future is now uncertain, and it would set my mind at rest if Harriet were to be happily settled with you."

"You are very kind, sir, and I do appreciate everything you say. Harriet has explained to me that the property is entailed to Adam Harford in due course, but my opinion is that we should not worry now about that eventuality."

"Then perhaps we ought to invite Harriet to come and join us in this conversation?" said her father, smiling.

"Yes, indeed, sir, of course. Shall I go and fetch her?"

He found Harriet sitting quietly in the library, doing nothing but looking out of the window at the pleasant lawn and gardens beyond.

When she saw him, she sprang up from her seat and he held out his hands to her. She embraced him and stroked his cheek softly in a gesture that was becoming delightfully familiar.

"What did he say?"

Fitzwilliam explained, and Harriet's expression relaxed into a warm smile.

Once they had rejoined Lewis Maitland in the drawing room, Fitzwilliam told them about the deteriorating condition of his cousin, Anne de Bourgh.

"Towards the end of my brief stay in Kent," he said, "the physician called to see her, and I escorted him back to his carriage as he left. I took the opportunity to enquire about my cousin's health in the longer term, as it seemed possible that he had not been able to speak freely in the presence of her mother, Lady Catherine."

"And what did he say?"

"He was very frank, Harriet. The young lady, he told me, will not live more than two or three weeks longer."

Lewis Maitland drew a sharp breath on hearing this negative pronouncement.

"I suppose," said Harriet, "that means we must not make any plans now if you will need to go south for her funeral."

Dialogue with Darcy

Fitzwilliam looked at her affectionately, and then made a decision.

"Rather, I would say that we should make plans. Your father has told me that he would like us not to delay. My own preference would be for a very small, friendly, family wedding with your two sisters, and my cousins from Pemberley, as the principal guests. For once, I share the view of my cousin Darcy. I would not want to have Lady Catherine at my wedding, for she is always a negative influence."

"But what about your brother, the Earl and the Countess from Essex?" asked Harriet.

"That is a difficult one to answer. I should like my brother and his wife to be present, but I do not know whether I can trust him to keep the matter private, and not pass on the information to Lady Catherine at Rosings."

"Perhaps you should seek the advice of your cousins Georgiana and Mr Darcy? They might be able to assist you."

Fitzwilliam agreed that he could do this, and said that they should ask Lewis Maitland's permission to tell the family at Pemberley about the happy news.

"Of course, sir, and Harriet wishes to write to her sisters, so that Julia and Sophie can be at the wedding with Kit and with Adam."

The discussion then moved on to details. Despite the sad association with the funeral of Harriet's mother, they agreed that the service should be held at the local church. Whether or not Harriet's close friend Emily Brandon should be invited was agreed to be left for further consideration. Other possible guests were Julia's father-in-law Harry Douglas, and his wife, maternal aunt to Julia, Sophie and Harriet.

Although Fitzwilliam had not made the journey to Banford Hall in any great apprehension of his suit being rejected, his frame of mind as he rode back to Pemberley was much happier and more settled, and the miles passed quickly as he returned to tell his cousins the news.

This was despite the fact that excluding Lady Catherine from the wedding was, for him, a major step. But now he had not only himself but his future wife Harriet to consider, and just using that term made him feel so very happy.

It was almost time for dinner when he returned to Pemberley, and Georgiana had arrived from her excursion to take Kitty to the Bingleys. So Fitzwilliam went upstairs to change before joining the family in the dining-room.

"And how are matters at Banford Hall?" asked Darcy.

"Everything there is very well, in particular, I have to press upon you an urgent social engagement in a few weeks' time."

There was something in the way he spoke that made Elizabeth look up, not in alarm, but as though the world had changed a little since she had last seen Fitzwilliam. Georgiana also heard a tone in his voice that gave her the feeling that her cousin had something very important to say.

"And what is that?" she said.

"A wedding," replied Fitzwilliam, "for I am very happy to tell you all that my dearest Harriet has agreed to become my wife, and Lewis Maitland has blessed the union and wishes us to marry as soon as may be."

Darcy was the only one of the three to be totally surprised at this answer. Elizabeth rose from her chair, and went across to embrace Fitzwilliam.

"Very well done, sir! That is very happy news."

Georgiana wanted to know why she had not been let into the secret, although she had had some suspicions. But Darcy was the one who demanded a full explanation, despite saying that he was very happy to hear the news, and it was high time that his cousin became a happily married man.

"Then if I may, I will tell you all about it."

When Fitzwilliam had finished his account of what had occurred that day, the plans that he and Harriet had for their wedding, and how his affections for her had developed during their visit to Yorkshire and since, Darcy expressed his surprise on one point.

"So you do not intend Lady Catherine to be there, whatever will have happened in the meantime? That is rather different to your usual compliant attitude where our aunt is concerned. May I ask why that is?"

"I suppose that I have decided that I no more wish that lady to interfere with my domestic arrangements in the future than you allow her to intervene in yours with Elizabeth. It will be better for everyone if I start as I mean to go on, and Lady Catherine is not a suitable arbiter of the relationship between me and my dearest Harriet."

"Forgive me for asking," said Georgiana, "but what will happen in the longer term, when Lewis Maitland is no longer living and at Banford Hall?"

"That is a perfectly fair enquiry, cousin. The honest answer is that I do not know. The house will then belong to Adam Harford, together with the income from the estate which pays for the upkeep of Banford Hall. But I have decided not to worry too much about that at the moment."

"Would you have enough to live on if you had to move elsewhere?" said Georgiana.

"I have a sufficient income, as you know, and Harriet will have the money from a small dowry, so I daresay that we should be able to manage in a rather smaller property. However I do not wish to upset my future wife by speculating about how long her father will live. Harriet is particularly anxious to stay with him at Banford Hall after we marry, and he is kind enough to be happy about that."

185

Dialogue with Darcy

"What do you think the attitude of her sisters will be to the marriage?"

"I am not sure, Darcy. I have not met either Julia or Kit Hatton although, from what Lewis Maitland has told me, they are both pleasant and sensible people. As for the Harfords, I have only been in the company of Sophie and Adam for a few days. I would have thought, since I have been told that theirs was a love match, that they would be content that Harriet should marry whoever she wishes"

Elizabeth smiled warmly at this, and said that that thought ought to be everyone's priority.

"Perhaps you should ask me that question in a few days' time, when there is a reply to the letter that Harriet has just written and sent to Yorkshire."

Fitzwilliam went on to repeat what the physician had told him at Rosings about the prognosis for Anne de Bourgh.

"She will die so soon!" exclaimed Georgiana.

"Yes, I fear so. So Darcy and I will have to travel south, and attend the funeral without telling Lady Catherine about my impending marriage. I am sure that my brother will be there, so I can decide whether or not to confide in him about Harriet and myself. The alternative is that he will hear the news after the wedding has taken place."

"Would you be inviting your friend Robert Harrison to your wedding?" asked Georgiana, with more than a vested interest in the reply.

"I certainly would like him to be with us, and I know that Harriet would also. Robert is planning, as you know, to visit us on his way to London, and that might coincide with the date of the wedding. We must wait and see what happens about that. It's quite surprising but, until one has to arrange such an occasion, you do not realise how many complications there can be!"

Dialogue with Darcy

As may be imagined, the next few days were fully occupied with discussing various arrangements. Georgiana went with Fitzwilliam to visit Banford Hall, where she received a very warm welcome from both Harriet and her father. She was able to keep Lewis Maitland company whilst Fitzwilliam and Harriet had some private time together.

"We have had a letter back from Sophie," said Harriet when she came back into the room with Fitzwilliam, "and another from Julia and Kit in Dorset."

"Oh! What did they say?"

It was Lewis Maitland that answered for both of them.

"As I had told Harriet would be the case, a few days' ago, they are all delighted at the news. Fitzwilliam clearly made a very good impression on Sophie and Adam in Yorkshire, and Julia and her husband are very happy to rely upon that opinion. They are already planning when they will travel to Derbyshire for the wedding. Julia and Kit will take the opportunity to stay at Norton Place with Harry Douglas and Lucy, who was my late wife's sister, and they will be bringing their small son with them who I have yet to see. Sophie and Adam will stay with us here until after the wedding."

With these and various other details to discuss, the time passed very quickly before Fitzwilliam and his cousin had to return to Pemberley.

There was still no news from Robert Harrison in Yorkshire, but on the following day a letter arrived from Kent for Elizabeth.

It was from Charlotte Collins.

"She writes to tell me that Anne de Bourgh was now gravely ill and not expected to last the week. At least," said Elizabeth, "we now know that Fitzwilliam and Darcy will need to travel quite soon to Kent, and will be back in plenty of time for the wedding."

Dialogue with Darcy

When Kitty returned from her short stay with the Bingleys, she was full of the delights and advantages of the house there. Charles Bingley had taken her on a tour of the grounds whilst his wife had been resting one afternoon.

"The gardens are not as spacious or as elaborate as the park is here at Pemberley, of course, but there are some charming copses and secluded areas for warmer days. Jane is looking forward to taking the new baby with her to sit on the lawn at the south side of the house."

Elizabeth thought that this would be an appropriate moment to tell Kitty about the sad news from Rosings.

"As you are due to return home soon anyway, Darcy and Fitzwilliam have suggested that you travel with them when they go to Rosings for the funeral. To stop at Longbourn to take you home is not a great deal out of their way, and you will remember that Mr. Fraser is planning to visit Hertfordshire before very long."

Elizabeth was interested to note that this last remark caused Kitty to blush slightly, but her sister was careful not to give a clue that she had observed this interesting sign.

"So I suggest that one of the maids should help you collect your things together, and arrange for any necessary laundry to be done, so that you are ready to travel at quite short notice."

The sad news, when it came two days later, was in a letter to Fitzwilliam from his brother the Earl, who had travelled to stay at Rosings to support their aunt. The funeral had been arranged for five days' time, so that Darcy and Fitzwilliam would be able to travel. It was agreed that they would take Kitty with them on their journey, and pause at Longbourn to deliver her back to her parents.

Fitzwilliam sent a message by one of the footmen to Banford Hall, to tell Harriet and her father the news whilst he and his cousin got ready to make the journey.

Dialogue with Darcy

Elizabeth had asked him to add that she and Georgiana would like to visit Harriet whilst he was away, if that would be acceptable, and Harriet sent a reply that she and her father would be very happy if they would do so, as she would like advice on some of the arrangements for the wedding breakfast.

Darcy and Fitzwilliam said a fond farewell to Elizabeth before they made sure that Kitty was comfortably settled in the carriage with them, and they went on their way. Before he left, Fitzwilliam had given an envelope to Elizabeth to be passed on to Harriet when she went with Georgiana to visit Banford Hall.

This invitation proved to be a welcome distraction from the rather sombre atmosphere at Pemberley whilst Darcy and Fitzwilliam were absent. Once Elizabeth and Georgiana had arrived at Banford Hall, Harriet took Georgiana upstairs to show her some new gowns that had been sent to her by Sophie from Yorkshire.

"How lucky," said Georgiana with a smile, "that your sister knows exactly what styles you like!"

"We used to argue about that when we were younger, but now I can accept that my sister has more opportunity than I do to see the latest gowns."

"But does she really know what suits you best?"

Harriet considered for a moment, and smiled ruefully.

"Yes, I have to admit that my sister the Duchess is very good at that. There are some colours that do not suit me, but Sophie rarely gets it wrong. I have protested once or twice about the expense, but she says that she can easily afford it from the generous pin money that Adam Harford gives her. Sophie says that I should make the most of her generosity for, once she and Adam have a family of their own, that will be the focus of her attention!"

Dialogue with Darcy

Meanwhile, Lewis Maitland had taken the opportunity to ask Elizabeth about the character of Lady Catherine de Bourgh.

"She is a very formidable woman," replied Elizabeth, "and not someone who I believe that you would welcome entertaining here at Banford Hall. I daresay that there are reasons for the kind of person that she has become, but my husband Darcy has always resented her attempts at interference, and especially her rude behaviour towards me before we were married. I can quite understand why Fitzwilliam does not want her to have anything to do with dear Harriet."

Her host nodded, but he still looked troubled.

"I do find it rather difficult," said Lewis Maitland, "that Fitzwilliam's brother the Earl may not attend the wedding, for he has no other relatives who are so close. I shall be happier if it is possible that he can come with the Countess and perhaps their children."

Elizabeth agreed with her host, and said that Darcy intended whilst he was in Kent to speak to the Earl privately about the matter.

"May I ask you directly," she hesitated, "whether you are happy about Harriet's choice of a partner? She is still quite young, and I assume that you have not put any pressure on her to marry?"

"You are quite right that there is no hurry as far as I am concerned, except that I had been worrying about what would happen to her once I am gone. But Harriet has always known her own mind and, now she has found someone who she truly cares for, I have no intention of standing in her way. I like Fitzwilliam very much, and doubt if there could be anyone else who I would prefer. I am very happy that they should marry, and marry soon."

"Harriet has spoken to me several times about your eldest daughter, Julia. Are they very alike?"

Dialogue with Darcy

"Yes, in some ways that is true, both in personality and appearance, whereas Sophie is more volatile and more like her mother in colouring and height. Perhaps your sister Jane is more like Julia? The eldest daughter in a family often has a more serious and responsible character."

Elizabeth smiled at this.

"Still, how boring it would be if everyone was the same! I am very happy now with all three of my daughters. Perhaps I had more in common with Julia before she married and moved to live with Kit in Dorset. But I have got to know Harriet much better since my wife died."

Elizabeth agreed with that, but explained that Lydia Bennet, the youngest in her own family, had always been the sister who had caused her the most concern.

After luncheon, when Mr. Maitland went upstairs to rest, the three young ladies settled down to detailed discussions about the wedding. Harriet showed them the dress that she planned to wear, and they talked about the wedding breakfast. Her aunt Lucy, married to Harry Douglas who had a house nearby, had offered to send over the cook and her staff from Norton Place to help, and that offer had been gratefully accepted.

"We have taken the precaution," added Harriet, "to ask my father's local physician, who is also a long-standing friend of the family, to be a guest at the wedding. That will be a comfort to me, in case the excitement of the day is not good for Papa's health."

That is very sensible, thought Elizabeth, and let us hope that his services are not needed.

The conversation moved on to Emily Brandon, who had been at her family's town house for some time with her aunt and uncle.

"Emily hopes to come back to Derbyshire next week, in time for the wedding, and so does her cousin Freddie. My sister Julia will be very pleased about that, for they all knew each other quite well when we were younger."

"Didn't you tell me," said Georgiana, "that there was some talk of Julia marrying Freddie's elder brother at one time?"

"Yes, my mother favoured that, and was enthusiastic about the prospect of my sister becoming a countess in due course. But Julia did not want to marry Dominic Brandon, and Papa agreed with her. Julia did not have eyes for anyone else once she had met Kit Hatton, and certainly the Earl's heir is a much less worthwhile person. I cannot believe that Julia would have been happy married to him."

"But you did," said Elizabeth, "gain a brother-in-law with a title later on, when Sophie married Adam Harford?"

"Yes, that's true, but that all happened some time after Mama's death. Sophie made up her own mind, and she only found out that Adam was the heir to his grandfather the late Duke after she had known him for some months."

Listening quietly to this conversation about romantic alliances reminded Georgiana of Robert Harrison and how she felt about him. It seemed to have been so long since Robert had returned to Yorkshire, and she was counting the days until she could see him again.

Seeing her sister-in-law look rather sad prompted Elizabeth to change the subject.

"My sister Jane and Charles Bingley are hoping that you can visit them, Harriet, before their child arrives. Perhaps there may be an opportunity for that after you return from your honeymoon? Are you and Fitzwilliam planning to be away for some time?"

"No, I do not believe so. We are going to spend a few days in Bath, staying at Aunt Lucy's house. I went to school in the city, but Fitzwilliam has only been there once, so that should be a very pleasant visit. I do not want to be away from Papa for too long."

"Will either of your sisters be here at Banford Hall whilst you are away?"

"Yes, Julia and Kit will remain here with their small son until we get back. My father will be very happy about that, as he has not been well enough to travel to visit the family at Morancourt."

In a quiet moment, Elizabeth passed on the envelope from Fitzwilliam to Harriet and that night, after the guests had returned home, she spent a happy few minutes reading his affectionate messages and endearments.

A day or so after Elizabeth and Georgiana's visit to see Harriet, a letter came for his daughter from Mr. Bennet. This gave a highly entertaining account of the arrival of Mr. Fraser at Longbourn, who had stayed for several days before moving on to his next task.

The engineer's constant willingness to discuss technical matters had not escaped his host, who found it necessary to absent himself at regular intervals to recover. However, Mrs. Bennet had been most impressed by the visitor, and the more so once she had realised that Kitty was the real reason for his journey.

"I must tell you, my dear Lizzy," wrote Mr. Bennet, "that a conversation between your dear Mama and that young man has never failed to entertain me, for she understands very little of what he is talking about, but he is endlessly anxious to impress her with the breadth of his knowledge. I wish that you had been here, but perhaps you have already had enough of hearing about all these technical matters.

In any case you are probably more interested in what I think of him as a prospective suitor for your sister's hand, for that is clearly why he has come to visit us. The answer must be that he seems to be a reasonable prospect for my daughter, since Kitty has quite simple tastes. She is pleasant without being a beauty, and has no special ambitions in life as far as I know. So I see no reason why she should not be as happily married to Mr. Fraser as to anyone else."

The last comment made Elizabeth laugh out loud, for she could just hear her father saying the words. That thought brought to mind her heartfelt wish that Papa lived rather nearer to Pemberley than he did. Then she realised that, in that event, Mrs. Bennet would also be much closer than she was now, which was not a remotely enticing prospect.

Mr. Bennet went on to inform Elizabeth that a second visit was planned by Mr. Fraser to Longbourn within the next week or two, when his prospective father-in-law confidently expected the engineer to make a formal proposal to ask for Kitty's hand in marriage.

That, thought Elizabeth, would make Mama quite the happiest woman in the world – if only for a few days.

Nothing had been heard from either Darcy or Fitzwilliam during their stay in Kent. Then, at last, two days' later their carriage came into sight, making its way up the drive towards the mansion.

Georgiana had left Pemberley earlier that morning at Emily Brandon's invitation to visit Cressborough Castle for luncheon, as the family had returned from London, so Elizabeth was the only member of the family to be there to welcome them home.

The travellers were tired and dusty from their journey but, after a change of clothes, they sat down with Elizabeth for luncheon and the chance to catch up with all the news.

"I have not been to a funeral for quite a while," said Darcy, "and had forgotten what a very sombre occasion it would be, especially for someone who died as young as our cousin Anne."

"Yes," added Fitzwilliam, "and that Reverend Collins has a most unfortunate manner of speaking which was of little assistance in the situation, at least to me!"

Dialogue with Darcy

Elizabeth could imagine exactly what he meant.

"Charlotte Collins asked me to pass on a message to you, my dear," said Darcy, "that she enjoyed her conversation with your father at Longbourn. I rather think that she may have been of more comfort to my aunt in her bereavement than all the portentous words that her husband could employ!"

Elizabeth was glad to hear that.

"How was your cousin, the Earl? Did either of you have any chance for a private conversation with him about the wedding?"

Darcy and Fitzwilliam looked at each other, and seemed to be rather unwilling to answer this enquiry, but eventually Elizabeth discovered that the subject had been discussed during both the journeys to and from Rosings.

"I regret that I eventually had to come to the conclusion that my brother could not be relied upon to keep a secret from Lady Catherine at this time, and Darcy shares that opinion. So I will write to him after the event, when we are staying in Bath, and take the consequences!"

Elizabeth knew that, although Fitzwilliam did not have as strong a bond with his brother as he did with his cousin Darcy, that still must have been a very difficult decision for him to make. But Harriet's happiness was clearly Fitzwilliam's only priority now, and no doubt the Countess, at least, would be supportive, as Darcy had once told Elizabeth that the Earl's consort had resented Lady Catherine's regular attempts to interfere in her household in Essex.

Once Georgiana had returned from Cressborough, she was able to update Fitzwilliam on the arrangements that Harriet had been making for the wedding in his absence. Her aunt Lucy would have arrived by now with Harry Douglas at Norton Place, and Julia and Kit Hatton, as well as the Duke and Duchess of Harford, were due very soon.

Dialogue with Darcy

"Georgiana and I have decided to keep what we are wearing a secret until the day, so please do not ask either of us!"

Darcy assured his wife that matters of that sort would not trouble him too much, whatever his sister might say.

As the appointed day drew near, Georgiana waited in vain for a letter to come for her cousin from Yorkshire, to say when Robert Harrison might be travelling south. The only mail that did arrive was for Elizabeth on the day of the wedding. She was with her abigail in her bed chamber getting ready to dress when a maid knocked on the door, to say that the post had arrived with a letter for Mrs. Darcy.

The writing on the paper was familiar. Charlotte Collins wrote from the parsonage at Rosings to say that Lady Catherine was awaiting the arrival of her nephew, the Earl, who was to escort her to Essex for a visit to his family. Meanwhile preparations were being made to close up the house after she had left, as though Lady Catherine did not anticipate being back at Rosings for some time.

However, the more significant news was in the next paragraph.

"I heard yesterday from my younger sister that Kitty is safely back home at Longbourn after her stay at Pemberley. She has told Maria that Col. Fitzwilliam is to marry soon in Derbyshire, to the daughter of a family known to you. Since Lady Catherine said nothing to us last night about that subject, when Mr. Collins and I dined with her at Rosings, I assume that she has not been told the news. If it is true, then I hope that you and Mr. Darcy are happy about the match. Col. Fitzwilliam is a very pleasant and amiable gentleman.

I will not mention anything on the subject to Mr. Collins, since he would be sure to pass the information onto his patroness immediately. However, it may be that Lady Catherine decides to travel on from the Earl's house in Essex to see you at Pemberley, although I sincerely hope that she would seek to advise you of any visit in advance."

Georgiana, having heard that a letter had arrived by the post, came to ask whether it might have come from Robert Harrison in Yorkshire. Elizabeth told her that it had not, and decided to keep the contents of the letter to herself for now, since she did not wish to spoil anyone's enjoyment of the day.

When Elizabeth and Georgiana, dressed in their best finery, reached the church on the wedding day, there was a small group of people waiting at the door.

Elizabeth recognised Sophie Harford, who came across to speak to them. She introduced Georgiana and Elizabeth to her sister Julia, and to the two gentlemen next to her. These proved to be Julia's husband, Kit Hatton, and his brother-in-law Adam, the Duke of Harford.

Mr. Hatton was a tall young man with dark hair and a pleasant manner. Julia Hatton had a strong facial resemblance to her youngest sister, although her golden brown curls were quite different from Harriet's darker and more disciplined locks.

They had a few minutes to talk before the groom arrived at the church with Darcy.

"My sister has written to me, Mrs. Darcy, to say how very kind your family has been to her and to our father. I have yet to meet Col. Fitzwilliam, but Papa seems to like him very much."

"Georgiana will agree with me, I'm sure, that there are not so many gentlemen of our acquaintance who are as fair minded and thoughtful as Fitzwilliam?"

"Yes, indeed, that is true. My brother Darcy and I are delighted that Fitzwilliam has met Harriet and persuaded her to marry him, for they seem to be so very well suited to each other!"

Dialogue with Darcy

Sophie Harford had been listening to this conversation with Emily Brandon, who had just arrived with her cousin Freddie.

"I understand that Fitzwilliam is happy to live with Harriet at Banford Hall after the wedding? In view of Papa's health, that will be a great reassurance for the rest of our family.

"The problem now will be," joked Emily, "that there are so few pleasant young men left now for other young ladies like me to marry!"

"That is not the difficulty," said Freddie, quick as a flash. "Your real problem is that a very special gentleman indeed will be required to keep you in order!"

Sophie Harford and Julia Hatton, having known the Brandon cousins for many years, were not surprised that this lively discussion continued for some time, until the sound of the wheels of a carriage could be heard on the gravel some distance away, and they all went in to take their seats in the pews at the front of the church.

Darcy had found that there had been no need to calm his cousin's nerves before the wedding, and Fitzwilliam's anticipation of the happy day to come had been sufficient to occupy his mind on the journey in the carriage, past Banford Hall to the village church. Once they had alighted, and walked up the nave of the church as far as the altar rail, they did not have long to wait before the bride arrived on the arm of Lewis Maitland.

So for everyone it was a very happy day, and Elizabeth was the only person there to have an uneasy feeling of what one unexpected visitor to Derbyshire in the next few weeks might bring.

During the wedding breakfast, there were many happy exchanges of news between the families and friends until, during a pause, the Duke of Harford rose to his feet to toast the bride and groom. Afar speaking a few well-chosen words, he reached into his pocket for an envelope containing some papers, and handed it to Fitzwilliam.

"This is a small gift from Sophie and myself on the occasion of your marriage. I had spoken to your father-in-law, Fitzwilliam, on the subject some days ago, so that he is aware of the contents. You and Harriet will both need to sign the documents in due course."

Harriet looked inquiringly at Lewis Maitland, but could not get any clue from her father's expression as to the contents of the envelope.

Fitzwilliam looked at Adam Harford blankly.

"Perhaps you should read out the beginning of the first document, so that everyone is aware of what it says?"

So Fitzwilliam began –

> *"I, Hector Cuthbert Ambrose Molyneux Harford, now known as Adam, Duke of Harford, hereby transfer in perpetuity all my rights to the inheritance of the property known as Banford Hall to my cousin Harriet (formerly known as Harriet Maitland) and her husband Fitzwilliam.."*

He was not able to read any further for the noise that came from the voices from the assembled company.

Harriet looked stunned, and quite unable to speak.

Her father Lewis leant across the table and pressed her hand in reassurance. Elizabeth looked to see Darcy's reaction, but immediately realised that the news had come as no surprise to him. Georgiana, sitting next to her sister-in-law, whispered in her ear.

"I did hear my brother discussing some legal matters with Adam Harford yesterday, but they stopped their conversation when they saw that I had entered the room."

Dialogue with Darcy

CHAPTER ELEVEN

It was the movement of the water that caught Elizabeth's attention as she looked out of the window in her sitting room. Georgiana was standing next to the fountain in front of the house, looking out across the lake towards the view of the hills beyond. But whilst her left hand beside her was still, her right hand was making a regular movement in the water, back and forth, back and forth.

After watching her for several minutes, Elizabeth came to a decision, and walked swiftly down the staircase to find Darcy in the library.

He looked up from reading the book of the estate's accounts, happy to have an interruption.

"What is it, Elizabeth? You look as though you may have come to a decision?"

That made it easier for his wife to tell him what she had come to say.

"Do you recall, my dear, the pleasant invitation that Sophie Harford offered to us at the wedding a few days ago?"

"Yes, I do. She seemed particularly anxious that we should visit them in Yorkshire quite soon, and take Georgiana with us."

"Yes, we spoke about the invitation on our return to Pemberley."

"You may remember that I said that, although Georgiana had clearly made a very good impression on the Duke and Duchess when she stayed with them a few weeks ago, we had never met the Duke, and the Duchess only briefly when she called here."

"Yes," said Elizabeth hurriedly, anxious to get to the point of their conversation, "but I have been thinking that I would really love to have a change of scene for a week or so, and soon. If we wait too long before replying to the invitation, I shall not wish to travel, for my dear Jane has only quite a short time now before her child is due to be born."

It was not that Darcy had forgotten about this impending event, but more that he had had other priorities on his mind.

"Yes, indeed, I do understand that you want to be here for that occasion and, as you have explained to me before, new babies do not always arrive when you expect them to!"

"Exactly, but I would like to accept the invitation now, if you do not object? I have not made an excursion of any length since we married, and I'm sure that Georgiana would not mind returning to Harford Castle."

Elizabeth did not go on to say that, in addition to offering the invitation, Sophie Harford had spoken to her privately that she had a special reason for suggesting that the Darcys should travel quite soon rather than delay.

The Duchess had not spelt out to Elizabeth exactly what this reason was, and she had not mentioned Robert Harrison in issuing the invitation, but it did not seem impossible that he might be connected with it. However, for the moment Elizabeth chose not to mention this thought.

"So may I write to Sophie Harford, and say that we will travel before the end of the week?"

"Very well, Elizabeth, if that is what you wish."

She smiled at her dearly beloved, and thanked him, before returning to her sitting room to write the letter to Yorkshire.

When Georgiana was told the news of the proposed excursion by her sister-in-law, a smile overtook her face for the first time to several days.

Dialogue with Darcy

"Oh, Elizabeth! That would be really delightful. I have been feeling rather down since Fitzwilliam's wedding to Harriet, and their leaving for their honeymoon in Bath."

Having imparted this news, Elizabeth went to find the housekeeper, to explain what was planned.

"I was wondering, Mrs. Reynolds, whether it would be a good idea for us to give the indoor servants a few days' leave to visit their families?"

"Well, ma'am, I would remain here with a couple of the maids and a footman, but we could put the covers on the furniture in the main rooms whilst the family is away. I am sure that the rest of the staff would be very pleased if you offer them that opportunity."

By this time, Elizabeth had grown to know Mrs Reynolds quite well, and they looked at each other for a moment and thought, but did not say, that Mrs. Darcy might have other reasons for wanting to close up the house for a few days.

Until the day came for the family to travel, Georgiana continue to look for the post each day, but no news arrived from Robert Harrison. Elizabeth wrote a carefully worded note to Lewis Maitland at Banford Hall, explaining that they would be away for a week or so, but would be in touch again on their return.

When he replied, Lewis Maitland said that Julia and Kit Hatton were still with him, and that he was very much enjoying getting to know his new grandson.

On the evening before the journey to Yorkshire was to commence, Elizabeth asked the housekeeper to come to her private sitting room.

"Mrs Reynolds, should anyone arrive at the house here at Pemberley whilst we are away, you will of course explain that the family has gone to Yorkshire. However, should any enquiry be made about Col. Fitzwilliam's recent marriage, or about his new wife, I hope that I can rely on your discretion to say the absolute minimum, and in particular not to refer in any way to Banford Hall or to the Maitland family."

Elizabeth knew that the housekeeper was very fond of Darcy's cousin, Col. Fitzwilliam, having known him since he was very young. Mrs. Reynolds looked puzzled for a moment, and then her expression changed to comprehension.

"I can assure you, ma'am, that should anyone, such as Lady Catherine, arrive unexpectedly, I shall of course be polite and offer her tea, but explain that the staff have been given a few days' leave. There would be no question of opening up the house for her to stay in your absence, whatever she might say!"

"I am pleased, Mrs. Reynolds, that we understand each other so well."

"May I venture to add, ma'am, that I hope that you hear better news of Mr. Harrison when you reach Yorkshire. I do not like to see Miss Georgiana pining as she has been these past few weeks."

Elizabeth thanked her and, as the housekeeper left the room, realised that it was good to know that someone who knew her sister-in-law so well had come to the same conclusion as she had.

When they retired to bed that night, Darcy ventured to ask a question that had been on his mind since his wife's original proposal.

"I have been wondering whether you might have had any other particular reason for wishing to accept the Harford's invitation straight away? Or are you going to tell me that there are some enquiries that a husband is not wise to make?"

Elizabeth considered this opportunity explain her reasons for wishing to be away from Pemberley for a few days, and decided that there was one that she would be safe to mention.

"You will recall that you had a letter from the Earl, your cousin, to say that Lady Catherine is staying with his family in Essex at the moment, following the death of her daughter Anne. What perhaps I have not mentioned is that Charlotte Collins wrote to me to say that your aunt might be considering an unannounced visit to Pemberley? Fitzwilliam did tell me that he planned to write to his brother from Bath to advise him about his marriage with Harriet Maitland."

"Oh!" said Darcy.

"Yes, and that would mean that your aunt would become aware of the match as soon as she reached your cousin's home."

"Yes. I would not put it past my aunt to just arrive here, seeking information, and no doubt intending to make trouble!"

Elizabeth smiled, and took his hand before replying.

"So perhaps you will now understand one reason for my wishing to be away from here for a while. I have spoken to Mrs. Reynolds, and asked her not to give any details about Harriet or where her family lives, should Lady Catherine arrive here and wish to find out that information."

Not for the first time, Darcy was full of admiration for his wife's ability to anticipate problems and think of a clever solution.

"And do you have any other reasons for wishing to travel to Yorkshire, my dear?"

"I believe that I would prefer not to answer that question for the moment. Can I ask you to trust me?"

"Provided that you suggest other ways for making up to me for any deception!"

Both Darcy and Elizabeth came to the view that these reasons for their journey should not be disclosed to Georgiana. So that all she was told was that the house was going to be shut up for a few days so that most of the staff indoors could make a rare visit to their families.

"That is a very fine idea," she replied, for Georgiana had a very kind heart and was always concerned to look after the people who served them at Pemberley. "I sometimes think that they get too few days of leisure in the year!"

Elizabeth was aware that Darcy was keen to make a good impression on their hosts when they arrived at Harford Castle, and so the family's best carriage had been polished to the highest shine, and the horses harnessed ready for the journey from Pemberley, with two of the grooms to act as outriders. Recalling the story that she had heard about the encounter that Sophie and Adam Harford had once had with highwaymen on the same journey, Elizabeth was pleased that they would have two strong young men to guard them should anything untoward befall them.

However, the journey was uneventful, although Darcy agreed with his sister that in parts the road was both uneven and badly surfaced. This time, it was Georgiana who was able to point out to them the first sight of Harford Castle.

"Look, there, can you see, the range of pale grey stone buildings, with the moat? When I was here before, I was told that the castle was built in the last century by the Duke's great-grandfather. The style pretends to be much older than it is, so the building has several towers, a drawbridge and all the turrets and arrow slits that a castle at least five hundred years older would have been furnished with."

Darcy and his wife could indeed see the castle, set against a backdrop of trees and admire the extent of the buildings and the attractive setting, and soon the carriage was turning into the drive and crossing the drawbridge. After they had alighted in the courtyard beyond, the coachman unloaded their baggage and then led the horses off through an arch at the side towards the stables. Darcy, Elizabeth and Georgiana approached the entrance doors, which were flung open before they could ring the bell. An elderly butler stood before them, who introduced himself as Somerville, and welcomed Georgiana as though she was a long lost friend.

"The Duke and Duchess are expecting you, Mr. Darcy, Mrs. Darcy and Miss Darcy. Please come with me."

Their hosts were sitting in the drawing room, and rose to welcome their guests. Soon the Duke was in a conversation with Darcy about the engineer, Mr. Fraser, and his work in the mines on the Harford's estate. Georgiana was drawn into this discussion, leaving Elizabeth to talk to the Duchess

"Now that you are here, Mrs. Darcy, there is something that I should mention to you. You and your sister in law may have been wondering why Robert Harrison has not made the journey through Derbyshire and on to London that he had been talking of after his mother's death?"

"I don't know whether Georgiana had been thinking about it, for she has said nothing to me. However, it is true that I had been surprised at his delay."

There was a short silence as the two ladies contemplated things that perhaps were left best unspoken for the moment.

"The real reason is that, following his mother's death, Robert was examining the family's accounts. Mrs. Harrison, although sadly physically restricted, was still very sharp in her mind, as Georgiana may recall, and so her son had left her to supervise the recording of the income from the property, which was dealt with by their estate manager. When Robert took over that responsibility, he discovered that there were discrepancies in the amounts received and dispensed."

"Oh!" said Elizabeth.

"Yes, and so Robert sought help from my husband, who sent over our estate manager from here to examine the matter. He reported to Robert, and later to us, that the man had been in post for about five years, and from the beginning had been transferring some of the income to buy property of his own elsewhere."

"What did Mr. Harrison do then?"

"Adam suggested to Robert that he should arrange to interview the man with my husband and our estate manager present. When confronted with what had been found, he admitted everything. Robert Harrison came to an agreement with him that, if the properties elsewhere were sold, and the money returned within a few months, he would not make the matter public. That would mean that the man could have an opportunity to obtain other employment."

"But that might, perhaps, mean that he could do the same thing elsewhere?"

"Maybe, although my husband Adam thought that Robert Harrison should be kept informed about where the man would be working in future, so that any further problems coming to light could be identified very quickly. As you may imagine, the whole matter has taken up a great deal of Robert's time during the weeks since his mother passed away."

So that is why, said Elizabeth to herself, that he has been too busy to travel to Pemberley to see any of us.

"Adam and I thought," said the Duchess, "that you all might like to meet Robert again whilst you are staying here, so we have invited him to dinner here tomorrow night and he has accepted."

This time, Elizabeth thought that she could be reasonably open.

"I believe that Georgiana in particular might be very pleased about that."

Sophie Harford smiled at her guest, but decided to say nothing.

"Perhaps I should add, "said Elizabeth, "that my husband Darcy is not aware either of what appeared to be Robert's interest in his sister, or that Georgiana might reciprocate that."

"And would you say that Miss Darcy knows anything about Robert's feelings?"

Elizabeth considered this, and hesitated to give a definitive answer to her hostess.

"He was a welcome guest when he stayed with us at Pemberley before he had to return home because of his mother's death, but I really do not know the answer to that. What would your opinion be about Mr. Harrison's intentions? I understand that your husband knows him well, and you also since you came to live at Harford Castle."

"I would guess that Robert may be hopeful, for they seem to have a great deal in common. Although he is very well educated and, as you may know, owns a considerable landed estate, he is not an arrogant man. Particularly now that his mother is no longer alive, Robert may be very keen to marry if he at last has found someone that he cares for. He has no surviving siblings, and is now living in that great house all by himself, with only a very handsome grand piano for company!"

Elizabeth smiled at the thought of a piece of furniture being a friend, but then remembered how content Robert Harrison had appeared to be, playing the piano at Pemberley with Georgiana. With that in mind, she had to agree with Sophie Harford that it might well be a match with a very happy outcome for both of them.

"May I ask how Mrs. Bingley is keeping? You must be very happy to have your sister living closer to you, now that she and her husband have moved house to Derbyshire? Harriet wrote to me some time ago to say that Mrs. Bingley is expecting a child soon."

Elizabeth acknowledged that that was indeed the case, and that the birth was expected within the next few weeks.

Dialogue with Darcy

That evening before dinner, the Duke took Darcy and Elizabeth on a tour around the main rooms in the castle, ending with the family's chapel and the pleasant walk alongside the moat.

Meanwhile Sophie Harford told Georgiana about the progress she was making with setting up a school for the children of the miners. That gave her the opportunity to mention that Robert Harrison had also started to renovate one of the buildings on his estate for the same purpose.

"How is Mr. Harrison?" said Georgiana rather shyly. "My cousin Fitzwilliam had not heard from his friend for some weeks before the wedding."

"I have not seen him recently, but my husband Adam took his estate manager over there recently because there have been one or two problems that Robert wanted some help with about the estate. But I understand that Robert himself is keeping well, except to having rather a lot to do after his mother died."

"Oh! I am sorry to hear that."

"You will be able to ask him yourself, Georgiana, for we have invited Robert Harrison to dine with us here tomorrow night at the castle."

I don't suppose that she is aware of it, thought Sophie to herself, but the expression on her face has just totally changed, to complete delight.

"He has been rather busy of late, but they are such good friends that I am sure Col. Fitzwilliam will not hold it against Robert if he has been rather occupied."

When everyone assembled later for dinner, even Darcy noticed that his sister was in a much more animated mood than recently. When an opportunity came, he asked his wife quietly if she knew of any reason to this.

"I would guess that the change of scene and seeing new people is making all the difference!"

On the following morning, Adam Harford went off with Darcy to look at the equipment that had been installed in his mines by the engineer Mr. Fraser. Meanwhile the three ladies inspected the buildings were being converted in the village to become the school for the children.

"This is all very spacious," observed Elizabeth. "What arrangements are you making the person to teach the children? Do you have someone locally who would be suitable?"

"Yes, I hope so, and that should all be arranged by the time the buildings are ready for use."

Georgiana was storing up in her mind all the details of the project, in the hope that Mr. Harrison might find them useful if he should ask her about it. She understood that the climate in Yorkshire could be quite cold in the winter, and wondered what arrangements would be made to keep the children warm. The Duchess was unable to answer that question, but said that Adam Harford had been discussing with his estate manager whether coal from the mines used in the fireplaces at each end of the room would be sufficient.

During the afternoon, Elizabeth and Georgiana went to one of their bedchambers to discuss which of the gowns that they had brought with them would be most suitable to wear that evening. Georgiana favoured her pale grey silk dress, which had an overskirt of lace.

"That is very fine, to be sure, but can I suggest that the blue dress with the embroidered roses is more becoming for your complexion?"

Georgiana debated the matter with herself, and finally decided that her sister-in-law was right.

When the two ladies made their way to the drawing room in the early evening, they were rather surprised to find Robert Harrison already waiting for them, in animated conversation with Adam Harford and Darcy. As soon as he saw them enter, the guest came across the room quickly and, after greeting Elizabeth, he turned to Georgiana.

"I may have made a nuisance of myself by arriving early, Miss Darcy, but I have been looking forward very much to seeing you. I owe you a profound apology, for I had intended to visit Pemberley again long since. Perhaps the Duchess may have explained to you that urgent problems have kept me at home for several weeks? How are you? I do trust that you are well."

And Robert Harrison bowed very low over her hand, a gesture which did not escape Darcy standing on the other side of the room.

Georgiana was initially overcome with confusion at her feelings in seeing him again, but she steadied herself and replied as calmly as she could.

"It is true that we had been hoping to see you in Derbyshire a while ago, but never mind, for now we are here. I hope that you are very well?"

Elizabeth then made some pleasant conversation with Mr. Harrison as her sister-in-law stood quietly beside her observing the gentleman of whom she had been thinking so frequently over the past few weeks. No, her memory had not played her tricks, and he was just as agreeable and as handsome as she had remembered.

"We are hoping," said the Duchess, "that after dinner Robert and Miss Darcy will favour us by playing the pianoforte in the ballroom. I have had it tuned especially for this evening; for I have heard how handsomely you play together."

"Oh!" said Georgiana, looking first at Elizabeth and then at her brother.

Darcy answered for them both.

"That is an invitation from your hostess that you must not refuse, Georgiana, and I hope that Mr Harrison will agree to join you!"

During dinner, Elizabeth realised how pleasant it was to see Georgiana looking so relaxed and happy again. Perhaps she and Darcy had been too busy with Fitzwilliam's affairs to notice how sad his sister had become recently. Darcy was occupied in conversation with Sophie Harford, so Elizabeth had the chance to speak with Robert Harrison without much interruption.

"Have you ever played on the pianoforte in the castle before, sir?"

He smiled and then said that he had to confess that he had been unaware that there was a pianoforte anywhere in the castle.

"I would guess that the instrument must have belonged to Adam's grandfather's wife, Leonie. She died quite young – Adam will tell you the story – and it is said that the late Duke was never the same man after that tragedy. The pianoforte has probably been stored away for many years. The instrument may have been found and the notes tuned for this evening, but I suspect that it may not be in very good condition after so many years of disuse."

Elizabeth smiled and said that no doubt everyone in the room would make allowances for that, and he agreed.

"As far as I know, neither Sophie nor Adam Harford plays any kind of instrument. The Duchess once told me that it is her younger sister, Harriet, who is the musician in the Maitland family. You were at her wedding, I believe? I was very sorry not to be there to see Fitzwilliam married for, as you know, he has long been a very dear friend of mine, but urgent and confidential matters kept me here in Yorkshire."

"Yes, Darcy said to me that something very untoward must have occurred to prevent your attendance. I hope that they will be very happy together. Lewis Maitland and Fitzwilliam seem to like each other, and Harriet living at Banford Hall after her marriage will be a good solution for everyone involved."

213

Dialogue with Darcy

Elizabeth wondered if Mr. Harrison would continue and say something to her about Georgiana, but he did not, and in some ways she was glad about that.

"Have you heard anything from Fitzwilliam's aunt, Lady Catherine de Bourgh? He has always seemed to be too tolerant about her interfering ways!"

"You will find that situation has changed considerably, for Harriet is his main priority now. Lady Catherine will have heard about the marriage after the event, which will not please her. My husband Darcy has never been willing to accept his aunt's attempts to supervise him, and it will be interesting to see what happens now that Fitzwilliam is taking the same approach. When I met her first, at her home in Kent, I found Lady Catherine overbearing, and unaccustomed to others stating their own views. However, I suspect that, as with other bullies, the answer is to be firm and stand your ground!"

He smiled at Elizabeth and agreed that her advice seemed to be very sound.

When the time came to move to the ballroom, even Elizabeth as a very amateur pianist could tell that Robert Harrison had been correct about the condition of the pianoforte. However, Georgiana and Mr. Harrison played well enough together to please their audience.

Elizabeth noticed that Darcy sat very still for the whole time that they were playing, and she suspected that he was not so much listening to the music as observing whether there was anything unusual about the way that his sister and Robert Harrison were behaving

When the time came for the visitor to return home, he asked Darcy and Elizabeth if they would like to visit him, bringing Georgiana with them. Darcy demurred, saying that he had an appointment with the Duke at the mines, but Elizabeth said that she and her sister-in-law would be happy to accept.

Dialogue with Darcy

When they reached their bedchamber, Darcy turned to his wife with a smile.

"I begin to be more aware of one of the other reasons why you thought it would be a good idea for us to visit the castle quite soon, my darling! Why did I not notice that before?"

"Perhaps you had too many doubts about a gentleman who can play the pianoforte, sir!"

Rather to her consternation, Darcy suddenly looked very serious.

"What is the matter, dearest? Have I said something to offend you?"

"No. Forgive me, the fault must be mine if I am as prejudiced as you seem to suggest. Only – I suppose that I have to realise that my sister is now old enough to make her own decisions?"

Elizabeth regarded him carefully before replying.

"You are, quite rightly, very fond of your sister. Perhaps you had some ideal image of who she might wish to marry, and Mr. Harrison does not fit that picture?"

Darcy was silent for what seemed to his wife to be a rather long time.

"No, you are, as so often, correct. Georgiana could, after all, have favoured some reckless gambler, or a military or a naval officer who would have wanted to take her far away from us, so that we rarely saw her, or any children that she might have."

Elizabeth hesitated and then smiled as she replied.

"So a handsome land-owning player on the pianoforte is not so bad after all?"

At this, Darcy's expression relaxed at last and a mischievous smile lit up his face as he held out his hands to his wife.

"You owe me some recompense for being so impudent, my darling!"

Elizabeth went across the room to him, and held his hands tight in hers. Then she whispered in his ear.

Dialogue with Darcy

"Tell me what it is that you want, and you may have it."

CHAPTER TWELVE

Mrs Reynolds was on the upper floor of the house, checking that all the rooms were tidy and in order, when she heard the sound of running feet before Amelia, the chambermaid, came into sight at the far end of the corridor.

"Amelia! What are you thinking of, rushing through the house like that?"

The girl's pace slowed to a decorous walk, so that Mrs Reynolds had to wait until she was close enough to talk normally.

"Now, what is it, Amelia? Have you done something wrong?"

"No, Mrs Reynolds. But I thought that you ought to know straightaway. There is a very grand carriage coming along the drive towards the house. I was in the drawing room, cleaning the windows as you had told me to do, when I glimpsed something moving in the gap between the trees. I'm sure it was a carriage! I wonder who it can be?"

"Well, let's see."

Mrs Reynolds walked across the room and looked out of the window. Amelia was right, for just visible on the drive across the lake behind the trees was a very grand carriage indeed, with two grooms riding behind it.

"Quickly, my girl, go downstairs and tell Thomas the footman to get his livery on immediately, ready to answer the door. And you had better go down and get your best apron, and then check that everything is ready for you to serve tea if necessary."

Dialogue with Darcy

Amelia turned, and moved as swiftly as she could along a corridor without actually running, and then down the stairs.

Meanwhile, Mrs Reynolds set aside her working apron, smoothed her hair and proceeded at a more decorous pace along the corridor and down towards the Hall. Amelia might not know who the visitor was, but the housekeeper thought that she recognised the carriage,

It was about five minutes before there was a firm press on the knocker, and Thomas emerged from the kitchen passage and, at a nod from Mrs Reynolds, opened the front door.

Standing there was a tall distinguished-looking gentleman who both he and Mrs Reynolds recognized. It was Colonel Fitzwilliam's brother, the Earl.

"Good morning, my man. I am here with Lady Catherine de Bourgh, who wishes to see her nephew, Mr Darcy."

Thomas replied that Mr Darcy and his family were not at home, and at that point Mrs Reynolds thought it prudent to come forward.

"Good morning, my Lord. I am sorry that Mr. Darcy and his family are away from Pemberley for at least a week, and we have sent most of the staff home for a few days and closed up the main rooms."

The Earl was briefly nonplussed at this reply, and then turned on his heel to talk to someone in the carriage behind him. Then he returned to speak to the housekeeper.

"Lady Catherine wishes to come into the house, Mrs Reynolds," he announced.

Mrs Reynolds drew herself up and took a deep breath. Then she replied,

"Can I suggest that I asked one of the maids to bring tea out to you on the terrace overlooking the lake, my Lord? I'm afraid that the drawing room is not available for Lady Catherine because Mrs. Darcy instructed us to put the covers over all the chairs and the rest of the furniture until the family return."

The Earl paused for a moment, and then said, "Very well, I will tell my aunt."

Mrs. Reynolds sent Thomas to ask Amelia to bring tea for the Earl and his aunt as quickly as possible, and then she went forward to wait outside as Lady Catherine to emerge from the carriage.

Her ladyship's uncompromising expression indicated that she was seriously displeased, but Mrs. Reynolds gave her a deep curtsy, and led the two visitors across the forecourt of the house and round the corner onto the lawn by the lake, where there was a table just the right size for two people to take tea sitting on the chairs overlooking the water.

When Amelia brought out the tray bearing the family's best silver teapot and service, these were accompanied by a choice of special biscuits which Cook always kept in hand. Amelia was trembling with nervousness as she lowered the tray onto the table, and so Mrs. Reynolds let her out of her misery and immediately sent her back to the kitchen.

The housekeeper poured the tea into the cups and laid out the plates for the visitors in case they might like to have a biscuit with their refreshments.

"And where," demanded Lady Catherine, "have the family gone?"

"Mr Darcy and his wife have gone with Miss Georgiana to Yorkshire, your Ladyship, to visit friends."

"Hrrmph," snorted Lady Catherine with disapproval. "And I suppose that my other nephew Fitzwilliam is somewhere else with his new wife?"

"I would have to ask you to refer any question about Col. Fitzwilliam to Mr Darcy, for I would not know the answer," replied Mrs. Reynolds.

Dialogue with Darcy

Lady Catherine was about to speak again, but then thought better of it.

The Earl took pity on the housekeeper, and suggested that she might like to withdraw whilst the visitors took their tea.

After about twenty minutes, the Earl came round the corner of the house into the Hall, where Mrs. Reynolds was speaking to the footman.

"Lady Catherine can see no purpose in waiting here any longer since the family are away, so she has returned to my carriage. Thank you for the tea and refreshments."

He paused, as though in thought. Then a small smile touched the corners of his mouth before he added, "You may tell my cousin Darcy that you did very well."

And he turned on his heel, joined Lady Catherine in the carriage and urged the coachman to drive on.

-0-0-0-0-0-0-0-0-0-0-0-0-0-0-0-0-0-0-0-

In Yorkshire, Darcy left early with the Duke to inspect the mines on the following morning, and Elizabeth and Georgiana had a light luncheon with Sophie Harford before leaving in the carriage to visit Robert Harrison.

When they arrived at the house, Elizabeth thought that Darcy should be suitably impressed at its size and furnishings. However, their host did not give them very much time to inspect the interior, but led them out onto the lawn where the hoops, mallets and balls for the game of pell-mell were already in place.

"In case you're wondering, Miss Darcy, these are not mine, but a new set that I have had sent from London for you to take back to Derbyshire!"

"Oh! That is so kind of you, sir - thank you!"

Robert Harrison smiled at her, but said nothing.

Dialogue with Darcy

"Well," said Elizabeth, "you must show me how to do this, Georgiana, for I have not had the opportunity up till now to play the game."

"Very well, let me see what I can remember from my last visit here," and, for the next ten minutes, her sister-in-law worked her way across the lawn pushing her ball through all the hoops.

While she was thus occupied, Robert Harrison had a quiet conversation with Elizabeth.

"Please advise me, Mrs. Darcy, for we do not have very much time without being overheard."

"Sir?"

"I am minded to ask your husband if I may make my addresses to your sister-in-law during your visit to Yorkshire. I have thought the matter over very carefully, but I would not wish to proceed without his consent."

Elizabeth explained that Darcy would be at the castle the following afternoon, because the Duke planned to discuss farming methods with his guest and his own estate manager present.

"So can I suggest, Mr Harrison, that you ride or drive over to the castle at some time after luncheon? I will find an excuse for my husband to have a private talk with you."

Robert Harrison smiled at her gratefully and thanked her, just as Georgiana rejoined them and invited them to join in the game.

For the next hour or so, Elizabeth found herself in the unusual role of chaperone, since her two companions soon started a conversation which appeared to be entirely decorous, but did not seem to require her to make any contribution. After a while, Georgiana realised this.

"Do forgive us, Elizabeth! It seems so long since I have seen Mr. Harrison, so we have found a great deal to talk about. This is a very handsome house, is it not?

221

Dialogue with Darcy

"Yes, indeed it is, sir. Fitzwilliam told us that you, like the Duke, are planning a school for local children. Is that far from here?"

"No, but probably too far to walk this afternoon. If you can spare the time later in the week, I know that the Duchess is very anxious to see how I'm getting on with the alterations to the building. I'm planning to open the school in about a month's time."

The rest of the afternoon passed pleasantly enough. Mr Harrison took Elizabeth on the tour of the main rooms in the house which were very handsome, with mahogany furniture and beautiful drapes at the windows.

Later, when the two ladies returned to the Castle, the butler Somerville met Elizabeth in the hall with a letter in his hand.

"This came for you this afternoon, Mrs Darcy."

Elizabeth thanked him, and went upstairs to read it. She had already recognized the handwriting; it was from her sister Jane Bingley.

When she got to the second paragraph she gasped, and then read quickly through the rest of the letter. Then she went quickly down the stairs, and asked Somerville whether Mr Darcy had returned from the mines with the Duke.

"Yes, ma'am, they returned about two hours' ago. You should be able to find his Grace and Mr. Darcy in the library."

Somerville was correct, and as soon as Darcy saw his wife's face he asked her what the matter was.

"Well, I suppose that nothing is the matter, but there is unexpected news from Derbyshire. Jane's child has arrived early, and I am now an aunt for the first time!"

"Congratulations my dear, and is it a boy or a girl?"

"Jane tells me that she has a healthy daughter, who looks just like her father!"

Dialogue with Darcy

Darcy observed with a smile that he was not sure that this was a very good idea. However, on second thoughts, a safe arrival was all that mattered.

"I do hope that you are not going to want to return to Derbyshire immediately, my dear, for I am enjoying my stay here at the Castle very much."

"No, of course not, for I agree with you. There is no hurry for us to return. Jane is being very well cared for, and we can look forward to seeing the baby next week when we get home."

Darcy then told her that he had just read a second letter that had arrived for them that day.

"Our housekeeper Mrs. Reynolds writes to tell us that there has been a visitation at Pemberley from my aunt, Lady Catherine, escorted by the Earl!"

Darcy could tell from his wife's expression that this news did not come as any surprise to her.

"Oh, what does she say?"

"As you had left precise instructions as to what Mrs. Reynolds should do, should that eventuality arise, she seems to have followed what you had told her to the letter. After taking tea with the Earl on the terrace overlooking the lake, Lady Catherine departed with a frown on her face, as you might expect."

Elizabeth smiled at this.

"My cousin the Earl left a message with Mrs. Reynolds for her to pass on to me, to say that she had done very well!"

"Are you unhappy with me, sir?"

Darcy took her hands in his and replied, "Of course not, my darling. I had not anticipated that my aunt would take the trouble to make the journey all the way from Essex to Derbyshire once she heard about Fitzwilliam's marriage. You clearly were much wiser. Would Mrs. Reynolds have told my aunt where Harriet's family resides?"

Dialogue with Darcy

"No, I had explained to her quite clearly why that would not be desirable. The last thing that any of us would want is that Lewis Maitland should have to be troubled by that belligerent lady. He is a sick man, perhaps with not too many years of his life remaining, and is delighted about Harriet's marriage."

Darcy did not reply, but took his wife into his arms and embraced her. When he released her, Elizabeth remembered the message from Robert Harrison that she had been asked to deliver.

Darcy's reaction surprised her. He turned his back, and for nearly a minute he said nothing. Then at last he looked at Elizabeth with a wry expression on his face.

"So I am to lose my sister to a gentleman from Yorkshire. You have been hinting as much, my dear. Will she accept him, do you know?"

"We have not discussed the subject directly, but I believe so. When in Robert's company, Georgina is a very different person now, and so much happier. But she will not marry without your consent, my dearest. You will not try to prevent the marriage?"

Darcy smiled at last, and his mood lifted.

"No. I shall miss very much having my sister with me at Pemberley, but that was going to happen, sooner or later. Georgiana and Robert Harrison seem to be very well suited, and it will do me no harm to travel from Derbyshire to Yorkshire – as often as we may be invited. He comes tomorrow, you say, to speak to me?"

Elizabeth smiled at him, and then held him close in her arms until they heard footsteps coming along the corridor.

-0-0-0-0-0-0-0-0-0-0-0-0-0-0-0-0-0-0-0-

That evening, the Duke has invited several local families to dinner to meet his guests, and Georgiana gave no hint of missing Robert Harrison. Elizabeth, sitting near her at the dining table, made sure that her sister-in-law was kept happily occupied by conversation, and escorted her to her room when it was time for bed.

When Robert Harrison came the following day to see Darcy, Elizabeth thought that his anxiety was clear, but her husband greeted him in a friendly fashion, and took him into the library.

Georgiana saw them pass across the hall together, so Elizabeth quickly suggested a walk around the castle grounds. Nothing was said between the ladies on the subject uppermost in their minds as they went along the side of the lake, but it was not long before Somerville the butler came to find them.

"Miss Darcy, your brother asks that you should join him in the library."

Georgiana looked anxiously at her sister-in-law for support, but Elizabeth smiled at her calmly before Somerville ushered the young lady across the grass into the house.

Elizabeth made her way towards the drawing room, where she found the Duchess about to take tea. It was not long before Darcy joined them.

Sophie Harford looked from one to the other but, for once, decided not to say what was in her mind.

They discussed the weather, the castle, and the new baby born to Jane Bingley in Derbyshire until the door opened, and Robert and Georgiana appeared together hand in hand.

No one needed to ask whether congratulations were in order, for one look at their faces confirmed that.

But after many words had been spoken, Robert Harrison said,

"I shall always remember that my happiness began today with a Dialogue with Darcy."

Dialogue with Darcy

Author's Notes

I do hope that you have enjoyed reading **"Dialogue with Darcy"**.

Details about my books can be found on my web site at **www.janetaylmer.com**

My first book about Jane Austen's hero Mr. Darcy is **"Darcy's Story"** – "Pride and Prejudice" from the hero's point of view. That novel is available as a paperback, as an illustrated book with more than 55 original prints, and as an ebook for downloading.

If you would like to read about Harriet Maitland's elder sister, Julia, you can enjoy her story in my book **"Julia and the Master of Morancourt"**, published by HarperCollins.

You can read more about what happened to Harriet's middle sister Sophie in my novel **"Sophie's Salvation"**.

If you would like to know about Jane Austen's life in Bath, you will find some information in my book **"In the Footsteps of Jane Austen through Bath to Lyncombe and Widcombe; a walk through history"**, which has many contemporary illustrations.

Best wishea

Janet Aylmer

Dialogue with Darcy

Printed in Great Britain
by Amazon

36247185R00136